WESTERN BAL
Ballard, Todhunter, 1903-
West of quarantine

1-08

WEST OF QUARANTINE

The hard crack of a rifle shattered the stillness of the hills, the bullet ricocheting off a rock near Bruce Powell's head. 'Ride back!' yelled Que Layton. 'I've got fifty guns covering you!'

There seemed to be no other way out, yet Powell hesitated. If he rode back, he'd be dooming Wirt Downer and his cattle herd to an ambush death. And it would mean ruin for himself, his brother, and the end of a dream to make Dexter Springs a cattle shipping center.

A cautious man would have obeyed the rough command, but Powell was through with running. Now was as good a time as any to make a final stand.

Todhunter Ballard was born in Cleveland, Ohio. He graduated with a Bachelor's degree from Wilmington College in Ohio, having majored in mechanical engineering. His early years were spent working as an engineer before he began writing fiction for the magazine market. As W. T. Ballard he was one of the regular contributors to *Black Mask Magazine* along with Dashiell Hammett and Erle Stanley Gardner. Although Ballard published his first Western story in *Cowboy Stories* in 1936, the same year he married Phoebe Dwiggins, it wasn't until *Two-Edged Vengeance* (1951) that he produced his first Western novel. Ballard later claimed that Phoebe, following their marriage, had co-written most of his fiction with him, and perhaps this explains, in part, his memorable female characters. Ballard's Golden Age as a Western author came in the 1950s and extended to the early 1970s. *Incident at Sun Mountain* (1952), *West of Quarantine* (1953), and *High Iron* (1953) are among his finest early historical titles, published by Houghton Mifflin. After numerous traditional Westerns for various publishers, Ballard returned to the historical novel in *Gold in California!* (1965) which earned him a Golden Spur Award from the Western Writers of America. It is a story set during the Gold Rush era of the 'Forty-Niners. However, an even more panoramic view of that same era is to be found in Ballard's *magnum opus, The Californian* (1971), with its contrasts between the *Californios* and the emigrant gold-seekers, and the building of a freight line to compete with Wells Fargo. It was in his historical fiction that Ballard made full use of his background in engineering combined with exhaustive historical research. However, these novels are also character-driven, gripping a reader from first page to last with their inherent drama and the spirit of adventure so true of those times.

WEST OF QUARANTINE

Todhunter Ballard

GUNSMOKE

First published in the UK by Rich and Cowan

This hardback edition 2007
by BBC Audiobooks Ltd
by arrangement with
Golden West Literary Agency

ISBN 978 1 405 68131 5

British Library Cataloguing in Publication Data available.

Printed and bound in Great Britain by
Antony Rowe Ltd., Chippenham, Wiltshire

1.

THE COMBINATION immigrant train of the Kansas, Texas and Southern labored its way through the blinding spring rain in a valiant effort to reach Dexter Springs before the whole uncertain roadbed should be washed from under its spinning wheels.

On both sides of the right-of-way the broken bluffs above the raging river were the only sign of solid ground. All the rest of the wind-lashed landscape had vanished beneath the surging course of the swirling flood waters, and the small, bell-stacked locomotive sprayed waves from its wooden cowcatcher as it forged forward, in constant danger that its firebox would drown out.

Inside the rattling coaches it was almost as damp. The train was already eight hours late and the wood for the heating stoves had long since been dissipated. The immigrant women huddled their crying children and themselves in shawls, hungry and cold and hopeless, already thoroughly disillusioned with this new bleak and barren land.

Joel Zeeman, the conductor, checking nervously through the train, halted beside Bruce Powell's seat, feeling the need to talk to someone he knew and someone who would understand the gravity of their situation.

"I tell you, Major," the little conductor removed his uniform cap and wiped his high forehead, "I never saw it so wet. The whole state is going to wash away if it doesn't stop raining. It's been pouring steadily since we left the Kaw, and it will be a miracle if we ever pull into the Springs."

Bruce Powell laughed. He was a man who laughed easily, although there had been little to provoke laughter in his life. He had worn a uniform at thirteen, and he had seen a beaten army surrender before he was twenty-one. The raw impulsiveness of his youth had been veneered by years of careful discipline and training, yet through it all he had managed to keep his balance and his perspective.

Even the hopeless drudgery of war and the empty bitterness of defeat had not marked him too deeply. He still had a

5

full-bodied zest for life, although he schooled it better than did his elder brother, and this schooling made men misjudge him at times, thinking that he was more serious than he really was.

He was calm now, and his laugh was friendly. "Cheer up, Joel," he said. "This is not the first time it's rained in Kansas, and let's hope that it will not be the last. Your train's crowded tonight. How many women you got aboard?"

The conductor returned his cap to his head. "Near a hundred and twenty," he muttered darkly, "and there's twice as many hungry young'uns. I swear, Major, seems everyone heading west has more children than livestock. The Lord knows how they'll manage to feed them. They'll wind up eating sandburs and brush if you ask me. It's those darned land agents' fault, lying and stealing, telling people they kin get rich overnight."

"Don't forget your railroad," Powell reminded him. "It's your cheap excursion rates that are filling up these trains and dumping a lot of hungry people into Kansas."

The conductor nodded unhappily. "These settlers don't know what they're up against. Them that don't drown out will dust out come summer. This land was made for cattle. It ain't never going to be any good for farming."

Powell's laugh was a little wry. "You sound like my brother Henry, but maybe you're both wrong. Maybe we'll live to see the day. . ."

He never completed the sentence, for the train jerked suddenly and then slid to a soggy stop. Zeeman swore under his breath. "Firebox. Water in the firebox. Now we're in a hell of a mess." He turned and ran down the aisle and disappeared through the car door.

Powell hesitated, peering through the rain-streaked window. Then he rose and started to follow. But as he stepped into the aisle his eyes met those of the woman in the opposite section.

He had remarked her when she entered the car at Dodge. In a train crowded with settlers her clothes were very noticeable, for they had been purchased in some city and she wore them with a certain dignity and ease.

But there was a nervousness in her manner. At first he assumed that she was unused to traveling, but after observing her for a few miles he changed his mind. He decided instead that she was frightened of something which she had left behind her in Dodge. As long as the train stood in the station yards she peered from the window, at the same time restraining the small boy who shared the seat with her. And even after they pulled westward she started up each time the car door opened.

She was, thought Powell, running from something. He had seen people who were running before. But what could this handsome gray-eyed girl be running from, and where was she running to? She must, he thought, be headed for Dexter Springs. There was nothing further west save the raw railroad work camps, overrun with their construction crews. Certainly she was not the type of woman to be going there.

As he stepped into the aisle the small boy was trying to crawl across the girl's knees. The child looked to be about four and there was a decided resemblance between him and the girl. Unconsciously Powell glanced at her ungloved hand and almost as unconsciously he noted that there was no wedding ring on her third finger. Then he realized with a start that she was speaking to him and the boy at the same time.

"No, Bobby," she said, pulling the child back, then meeting Powell's eyes. "There's no serious danger, is there?"

Powell smiled. He was almost as dark as an Indian, and his teeth showed white against the black sunburn of his lean face. "I don't think so. The roadbed's solid and should hold, even if we're delayed for a while. I'm going forward to find out."

He moved on down the aisle, thinking more about the girl than about the stalled train. He had just grasped the knob, preparing to pull the car door inward, when it was thrust open in his face.

He stepped back to avoid its swing and the doorway was filled by the bulk of the entering man.

The man was short and squat, entirely sheathed by a dripping black slicker, and his soggy hat was pulled down so that it shaded his eyes. But it wasn't the hat which held Powell's attention. It was the handkerchief tied across the lower part of the man's face and the heavy gun in the man's hand.

Powell's own weapon was in his valise, but had he been wearing a gun belt he would have had no chance to draw. The man was almost on top of him.

"Steady." The man's voice was partly muffled by the handkerchief, but it was still a roar. "Back up into that seat."

For a moment Powell hesitated. Then he eased into a seat space already occupied by an immigrant woman and two small children.

A second masked man had appeared in the doorway behind

7

his companion, and the bulky gunman passed Powell, shouting in his bull-like voice, "Everybody stay where you are and you won't get hurt. This is a holdup."

Powell twisted to watch the man's progress down the car, and tensed as the bandit paused beside the gray-eyed girl. She started to stand up, her face blank with alarm. He pushed her roughly back into the seat and, reaching across, seized the small boy, lifting him bodily by the collar of his jacket.

The girl grabbed at the man's arm. He put an elbow into her face, shoving her away roughly. Powell forgot the gunman in the car door. He plunged into the aisle, jumping instinctively toward the gunman who was backing along the car, the struggling boy under his free arm.

But the bandit behind Powell was quicker. He charged after the major, one of his heavy forty-fours coming up in a swing. Then he crashed the six-inch barrel down across the flat crown of Powell's wide hat.

Bruce Powell dropped to his knees. He caught the arm of the seat at his side and tried to drag himself erect. The heavy gun struck again and then again. Powell collapsed, first back to his knees and then forward onto his face. He lay there unmoving, his cheek pressed against the mud of the dirty floor. The bandit stepped across his inert body and carried the boy from the car, his departure covered by his companion.

2.

CONSCIOUSNESS RETURNED slowly to Powell. He felt the uneven jolting of the moving train and then managed somehow to open his heavy eyelids. Joel Zeeman was bending over him, his thin face dull with worry.

"Sure, Major, I thought we'd lost you. They beat the top of your head to pulp."

Powell closed his eyes, trying to concentrate on Zeeman's words. Then he remembered. "The boy," he whispered. "What happened to the boy?"

"They stole him," said Zeeman. "There were five of them

and they set lanterns at West Bridge. Johnson figured that the bridge must have gone out and stopped."

Powell tried to keep his eyes open and failed. He tried to sit up. His head spun, and then he sank back into semi-consciousness on the piles of blankets at the end of the baggage car.

The next he knew cool fingers touched his forehead and he opened his eyes to see the girl's face above his. He heard her soft voice. "The conductor thinks you're better. He wants you to lie quiet. We'll be in Dexter Springs very soon."

Powell dozed, only to rouse a third time with the confused knowledge that the train had stopped, that they were lifting him through the car door and carrying him across the dripping platform to Steve Foster's station hack.

Then he was on a narrow hotel bed in one of the Dexter Springs House's better rooms and could smell the odor of whiskey as Doctor Horndyke bent above him. Horndyke was a short, heavily bearded man, sarcastic and capable.

"Well, well." The doctor seemed to be reasonably sober. "You sure got a dent in your skull, Major, a very pretty dent indeed."

Powell grimaced and said weakly, "I don't need a doctor to tell me that."

"Of course not," said Horndyke. "Of course not. None of you people in this blasted country ever think that you need a doctor until you're dead, and then it's too late. What day is this?"

Powell thought slowly. "Monday," he decided.

"How old are you?"

"Twenty-four."

"I guess you'll do. Did you get a good look at the bandits?"

Powell moved his head painfully sidewise. The movement made him a little dizzy. "They had on slickers," he said weakly.

"They needed them." Horndyke chuckled without humor. "And their horses must have had gills. Never saw so much water. They must have wanted that boy badly to come out on a night like this. Silly thing, to hold up a train just to grab a child. Too many children in the world anyhow. Every soddy for miles ahead is filled with them."

Powell's attention was wavering, but Horndyke kept on talking. "Handsome-looking woman. Haven't seen a female that could hold a candle to her for years. Child's mother?"

9

Powell mumbled, "I hadn't a dozen words with her. I don't know."

Horndyke chuckled again. "Now, isn't that like a Texan, jumping in to protect a woman he doesn't even know and getting his head split in the bargain!" He turned away from the bed, filled a glass with water from the pitcher on the stand, then shook a white powder into it.

He came back to the bed, thumbed Powell's eyelids out of the way and looked at the pupils. Then he put a hand under Powell's neck. "Come on, drink this."

Powell struggled to sit up. "What is it? Will it cure me?"

"It will make you sleep." The doctor sounded irritated. "Nature will have to cure you—nature and rest. A doctor merely helps nature effect a cure." He lowered Powell back to the pillow, smoothed the covers, turned and, picking up his bag, moved over to blow out the light. Bruce Powell was asleep before the doctor closed the door.

3.

JENNY PARAINE had never felt so utterly alone and friendless in her whole life. She stood on the windswept station platform and watched them lift Bruce Powell into the station hack. Then she looked uncertainly around.

Joel Zeeman came over to her side. Joel felt that in some way the railroad was to blame for the holdup, and as the representative of the line he conceived it his duty to do anything that he could to aid this girl.

"There's not much law out here, ma'am," he told her in a subdued voice, "and mostly people are rough and ready as you might say. But Kansas people ain't child stealers, no sir, and they won't take kindly to the news, I promise you."

"Please," she said. "I . . ."

"You come right along." He gathered up her baggage. "Hack will be back in a minute. I'll take you to the hotel and then round up the deacon. The deacon ain't old, but he's made quite a name for himself in this country. The deacon was in Ellsworth and Cottonwood and Dodge. He's marshal here, and he's honest after his own lights, which is more than

10

you can say for all law officers. The deacon will help you get your boy back if he can."

She waited in the hotel lobby while the small conductor went to round up the deacon, and she was as near despair as she had ever been in her twenty-two years.

Dear God, she thought, *he means to help. They all will probably mean to help, but I haven't got a chance. I should have known it before I came west. I should have known it before I took Bobby out of Dodge City. I'm beaten, but I can't leave. I'll have to stay here somehow and do what I can. Bobby must be close. Those bandits couldn't have ridden far in the rain. I hope they covered him. I hope he didn't get soaked. I hope he doesn't get cold.*

By the time Zeeman returned she had gained control of her feelings. Zeeman brought not only the marshal, but Lenard Milliard who owned the Springs' largest store and Andrew Hyde, the mayor. They were joined a moment later by John Kleban, who owned the hotel, and she had time to study them as she was introduced.

Deacon Sandson was young and ambitious and stubborn. The mustache which he tried doggedly to grow was thin and silky and without much color or body. His hair was yellow and he wore it close-clipped, so that his evenly formed round head showed pinkish and clean-looking at the roots. His eyes were amber, round and solemn. He was a man without humor, who took all things seriously.

He had come to the Springs at Andrew Hyde's request, and his ambition was to make himself the most powerful man in western Kansas.

He listened carefully to the account of the train holdup, first from Zeeman and then from the girl, and when they finished he shook his head slowly.

"I don't know." His odd eyes were on Jenny's face and his stare made her uncomfortable. "This rain will wash out all tracks, of course."

Andrew Hyde fussed nervously with his heavy watch chain. As mayor he felt that the town's reputation was at stake, and the fact that a pretty woman was involved only made things worse.

Hyde had all the instincts and weaknesses of a politician. He too was ambitious, and he was not above using the marshal to further his own ends, but still he felt a real sympathy for this lonely girl.

"It was a queer holdup," he said slowly. "They made no

effort to rob anyone. They just took your boy. That would lead us to think that it was engineered by someone known to you—your husband perhaps?"

"I have no husband." Jenny spoke before she thought, and saw the misunderstanding grow in their eyes. "I mean . . ." She tried to correct her mistake. "I mean I have no husband now . . ." She let her voice trail off. She was a person who hated lying, and would go to great lengths to avoid false-hood.

But what could she tell them? Her eyes searched their faces. Whom could she trust? Her voice broke. "I'm very tired. I thank you for your help, but there's not much can be done in this storm and . . ."

She felt them draw away from her. She knew that they guessed she was not telling the full story. She wanted them to go, to leave her alone. John Kleban sensed this and stepped forward.

"Of course you're tired. I'll show you to your room." He got a key from behind the box desk and carried her bags up the open stairway. She followed, but halfway up she looked back at the lobby, and found that Sandson's eyes were on her—intent, amber, glowing up at her in the half-darkness of the stairs, reminding her of nothing so much as the eyes of a hungry cat.

She shivered and, turning, hurried after the hotelman. Not until she stepped into the room where John Kleban had already lighted the lamp did she stop shivering.

The hotelman checked the towels and made certain that the flowered pitcher on the washstand held water. Then he turned to his newest guest. "Is there anything else?"

"A question," said Jenny Paraine. She had already removed her scuttle hat and laid it on the white bedspread, and her hair showed soft and warm and golden under the lamp-glow. "Is there any work for a woman in the Springs? I've had very little training, but I can cook and I'm not too bad at sewing and . . ."

John Kleban was forty-eight years old, and thirty of those years had been spent in sizing up hotel guests. He felt that he was as good a judge of character as any man alive, and he had tried to judge the girl ever since she entered the hotel lobby. There was something appealing about her, yet something strange, as if she had known deep trouble, tragedy perhaps. Yet whatever shadowed her had not made her bitter.

He ran his square hand through his thick black hair, considering. "Ma'am," he said, "if you'll pardon my saying so, Dexter Springs is not the place for you. A year ago this town was just a railhead camp and it's still rough. We hope the Texas herds will drive in here, and if they do it will be hell on wheels. Go back where you come from."

"I can't," she said, and gave him her small smile. It was a smile, thought Kleban, that would melt the wooden heart of a cigar-store Indian. "I've got to stay here." Her voice was low, yet full-bodied with no trace of whining. "Bobby is here somewhere. Those bandidts can't have taken him far. I've got to find him, and I have very little money."

Kleban hesitated. "I hate to offer it," he said slowly. "It's not quite a fit job for a lady like you, but I've been looking for someone to run my dining room."

Hope leaped into her gray eyes, and her face softened with its relief. "You . . . you actually need someone? You aren't making up a job merely to help me?"

John Kleban looked at her. He was noted as a hard man at a poker table and a close man with a dollar. He rather prided himself on both reputations, but, as he told the mayor later, "Darned if I wouldn't have built a dining room and turned it over to her just to see the way the light came up into her eyes. I never met a woman like her before. I don't expect to ever meet another, not in my whole life."

"Ma'am," he said when he recovered, "I can't recall exactly when I did my last favor for anyone, and believe me, I am not doing you a favor now. I guess the boot is on the other leg. With you running the dining room every other eatery in town will likely have to close, and those aren't just sugar-coated words. I mean it."

"Thank you," she said, and, coming up on tiptoe, kissed his leathery cheek. There were tears in her eyes, but she smiled through them. "You're one of the nicest people I have ever met, and the Springs is one of the nicest places I have ever been."

John Kleban gulped. There was something of retreat in the way he backed through the open door. She followed him, and as she stepped into the hall the bearded doctor came from the next room, carrying his bag.

Kleban welcomed his appearance with relief. "How's the major?" he asked quickly.

Horndyke's bold, bloodshot eyes examined the girl with open curiosity before he answered. "The major will live," he said without too much interest.

13

Jenny Paraine's question was almost sharp. "How seriously is he hurt?"

Horndyke took his time to answer. "His brains are slightly scrambled. A man's head was not made to be beat upon with the barrel of a heavy gun. We call it concussion and don't know too much about it, but he'll recover. Nature will heal him if he stays quiet."

"And if he doesn't?"

The bearded lips quirked. "Then Nature will probably heal him anyway. She's pretty good at healing, Nature is. And the major is young and he's strong as an ox, whipcord and muscle. You get that way from living in the saddle." He glanced at her keenly, noting the shadows under her eyes.

"You could use some rest yourself. Let me give you a powder."

She shook her head. "I'll sleep," she promised.

He gave her another appraisal, shrugged and turned to the stairs down which Kleban had already disappeared. Jenny Parlaine was motionless until he had gone. She started to turn back into her own room, hesitated, and instead tried the knob of Powell's door. It turned under her hand and she pushed it quietly open.

The light from the hall behind her showed her the sleeping major and she moved forward until she stood above the bed. There was a white bandage above the left temple where the slashing gun barrel had bashed the skin, and his sunburned face had lost color until it was not too much darker than the bandage. He looked drawn, and yet very young, like a child who has been hurt, and she knew a quick start of emotion.

"Why, he's not much more than a boy. I thought he was older, much older." She stood studying the face. Even in repose it showed determination and strength. Perhaps it was the bone structure, the squareness of the jaw, the way his mouth tightened at the corners. It was the face of a dominant person, a person born to command, and yet there was nothing cruel about it.

One hand lay outside the blankets, square-fingered and capable. On impulse she reached out and touched it lightly. Instinctively she knew that she could turn to this man for help, and she needed help so very badly. She was near the end of her strength. She had tried fighting alone and she had failed. But did she dare trust him? Did she dare trust anyone? It was something which she couldn't answer. She turned slowly and went out, closing the door softly behind her.

14

4.

IT WAS the third day after the holdup before Bruce Powell left the hotel room. The rain had stopped, but the empty plain was still a sodden mire, and the town huddled damp and desolate, waiting in dreary patience until the wan, chill sun should suck the wetness out, or the unobstructed wind would blast it away.

The lobby was deserted and Powell crossed it to step out onto the gallery, turning up the collar of his brush jacket against the rasping air. He stood for a moment looking about, then followed the new boardwalk past Len Milliard's store to the raw frame building which housed the *Enterprise*. Turning in, he found Cap Ayers before the type case, breaking down the forms.

Cap Ayers was short and his girth was so great that he resembled a small balloon. His shoulders were wide and his neck was almost nonexistent, his head warting up directly from his shoulders, bald and pink and shining like a polished mirror.

Between these two men was a comradery of deep and perfect understanding, an unlikely friendship, perhaps made stronger by the divergence of their natures, and Bruce Powell understood that Cappy gave him a fondness which the printer reserved from other men.

There was a smudge of ink across one of Cappy's oversized ears, and Powell sometimes wondered if the printer ever really washed. There had been such a smudge upon that ear the first time he had seen the fat man.

"Well," said Cappy, without turning or interrupting his work. "I'd begun to think you'd retired to bed for good."

"That damn doctor." Bruce Powell grinned as he picked up a blotted copy of the previous day's paper and glanced through it. "He doped me, and he kept doping me. I'd have spent the rest of my life in that bed, but I came to enough this morning to realize what was going on and poured my breakfast coffee out of the window. 'Sleep,' Horndyke kept telling me. 'Sleep and Nature will heal you.' The drunken sot."

Cappy grinned as he unlocked another form and his flying fingers broke up the type, dropping each slug into its proper place in the case.

Powell leaned against the high counter and ran a quick eye over the newspaper. Then he opened the four-page sheet and inspected the center truck. "What's this?"

Cappy wiped his ink-stained hands on the seat of his butternut trousers, carefully avoiding touching his apron, and came around the counter belligerently. "What's what?"

Powell folded the paper open and read:

$100.00 REWARD

The Dexter Springs *Enterprise* will pay $100.00 in gold to anyone furnishing us with information regarding the whereabouts of the four-year-old boy, answering to the name of Bobby, who was stolen during the train holdup at West Bridge on last Monday night. All communications regarding the boy and his present whereabouts will be treated in the strictest confidence, and the informant will be fully protected.

Bruce Powell
Publisher

Powell looked at the fat man. "Who wrote that?"

Cap Ayers took time to spit into the tin can at the end of the counter. "Who usually writes this paper, and prints it, and circulates it?"

"And who gave you authority to offer a hundred-dollar reward?"

"Keep your hair on," said Cappy. "It ain't your money we're offering. The girl brought it in in gold and asked me would I run the notice, and would I sign it like it was the paper who was trying to locate her boy, and what was I supposed to do?"

The major grinned. "What you did, you old fraud, only you should have told her to keep her money. We'll pay the reward."

Cappy spat again. "Sure and that's exactly what I told her. I said, it's a crying shame, little lady, when women and children ain't safe, a-traveling on our railroads, and the major will take it kindly if you allow him to pay the reward money when it's claimed."

"And has it been claimed?"

Cappy shook his head. "Ain't hide nor hair been seen of that boy. He's probably hidden out in some soddy. Town ain't talked of nothing much else, but we don't know nothing more than we did, and we don't know much more about the girl either."

"What's she like?" Powell was curious.

"Like all females," said Cappy. "A woman talks a lot and never says much about herself. A man talks little and tells you everything. You'd have thought she worked on a newspaper, the questions she asked."

"Questions?"

"About the town, and the people in it, and she wanted to know all about you."

"Did she?"

"She did that."

"And you told her nothing, of course."

"Well," said Cappy, spitting again and wiping his full lips with the back of his broad hand, thereby adding a new streak of ink across one fat cheek, "I did and I didn't. I told her that she should watch out for you."

"For me?"

"For you," said Cappy. "I told her you was a tomcat and that all the girls from here to the gulf was wild about you."

"You lying old reprobate."

Cappy grinned. "Well, they should be. At first she wanted to know how old you were, and I told her, and then she said that you were pretty young to have been a major and I told her that all the better men had gotten killed and the Texas Brigade was plumb out of officers. I sure wish a good-looking female was asking questions about me and I had a flannel-mouthed friend to give her the right answers. Believe me, Major, she thinks you're a cross between Jeb Stuart and Robert E. Lee. Never does a man harm to be built up a little to a woman."

"Cappy," said Powell, "the truth isn't in you. You love to lie."

"Hell," said Cappy, "what's the fun in telling the truth? Any damn fool can do that. But I told her some truth. I said you rode out to fight the Yanks at thirteen, and I told her you were a major before the end because all the better men had been killed."

Powell moved restlessly, all his humor gone. "And that's nearer the truth than even you know."

17

Cap Ayers ignored him. "And I told her that you and your brother came back to Texas and found it filled with cows and no money. That you gathered a herd and drove to Missouri and lost them to the jayhawkers. That you went back to Texas and gathered another herd and brought it into Dodge."

Powell was watching him sardonically. "Did you tell her how I got this newspaper?"

"That I did," Cappy grinned, "and she laughed when she heard the story. She can still laugh although she is eating out her heart with worry about the boy."

"And nothing has been done to find him? Where does she come from, Cappy?"

"That I don't know. She's friendly and polite, but she acts scared. She doesn't talk about herself. When I tried to question her she side-stepped and weaved like a half-broken horse, and by the time I finished I knew little more than I had when I started to talk."

Powell considered. "At least you know her name?"

"Paraine," Cap told him. "At least that is what they are calling her at the hotel. But I have not seen any Mr. Paraine and she seems to hesitate over the name."

Powell straightened, the humor entirely gone from his face. "Cappy," he said, "you just told me that you know nothing about this girl. Stop implying that she is something that she shouldn't be."

"Hold up." Cappy came around, his full face almost purple with quick anger. "You're a fool, Major, reading into my words something which I did not mean. She's probably married. The boy is probably hers, but I doubt if the name Paraine belongs to her legally. I think she is hiding her identity for reasons of her own."

Bruce Powell stared at him for a long moment. "Have you any real reason to believe this?"

Cappy shook his head. He was still angry, but the color was gradually fading from his face. "None in the world, except I am an authority on women. I have been married five times, and a man can't go before a preacher that often unless he understands females thoroughly. It's the way she acts, the way she talks, the way she doesn't talk about herself."

"Cappy," said Powell, "are you suggesting that she is a criminal?"

Cappy stared at him, then he laughed. "Of course not.

She is the prettiest, sweetest, most lovable girl I have seen in years. But judge for yourself if you can get close enough to speak to her. Every man in town is buzzing around her like hungry flies. Some think her husband is dead and the field is open. Others don't care. But they are all interested.

"Even John Kleban has taken to wearing white shirts, and I never thought John had anything warmer than river water in his veins. And Deacon Sandson is strutting about in new polished boots, wanting to shoot anyone who dares to smile at her. The Deacon has got it bad, and when a man like Sandson sets his mind on a woman, there is bound to be trouble."

The major was contemptuous. "Sandson is a fool."

"Is he?" said Cappy, and did not grin. "A woman raises hell with any group of men, especially if she is a good woman. Go ahead, pretend that you weren't impressed by her on the train. Which brings up a point of great interest. Just who was it that held up that train?"

Bruce Powell said slowly, "I can't be sure, Cappy. The men were done up in their slickers until their own mothers wouldn't have recognized them. But the bull voice . . . I'd heard it before, and the man knew me. I could see it in his eyes. I'd say that it was one of the Layton boys."

Cappy swore. "You sure?"

"If I was sure," said Powell, "I'd be riding out there right now. Of course I'm not sure."

Cappy shook his head slowly. "I don't get it. What would the Laytons want with that boy? What would they have to do with the Paraine girl?"

"Don't ask me. I don't know."

"What are you going to do about it?"

"I don't know that either," Powell said. "Right at the moment I'm going back to the hotel and have a look at her, and get a bite of lunch in the bargain." He turned and moved out of the print shop.

5.

OUTSIDE THE door he paused to light his first cigar in three days and let the growing warmth of the noon sun seep through his big body as he looked slowly over the town.

It was as yet not too much of a place, but he had taken a hand in its building and he had a deep proprietary interest in its uncertain future.

He had been away three weeks and even in that short interval the place had grown. Then, raw buildings were filing up the gaps along the street, making it look busy and important; yet the street itself was nothing but a sea of sticky mud, and the slatted sidewalks were little better, for the damp steaming boards had been so tracked with goo from the roadway that the footing on them was almost as treacherous as in the center of the rutted thoroughfare.

The town lay roughly in the form of a dumbell; two towns, in fact, connected loosely by the disordered collection of buildings straggling along State Street and Kansas Avenue between the railroad station and the new grange hall.

The new residential section was huddled beyond the grange hall to the north, while to the south the older portion was crowded about a crisscross of twisting alleys. This section below the tracks was a holdover from the railroad construction camp of the preceding year, a sorry collection of cheap saloons and cheaper dance halls.

Above it, along the tracks, were the new loading pens for the stockyards which Powell and his brother had built to receive the expected trail herds which they hoped were pushing northward from the Red River Crossing.

If the herds ever arrived, if the grangers did not keep them out of Dexter Springs, the Powells stood to make a comfortable fortune. If they had guessed wrong, if the herds never came, they would lose everything they had in the world.

Powell turned slowly up the street toward the hotel, his mind busy with many things. But as he passed the open double doors of Lon Milliard's store he glanced into the semi-darkness of the cluttered room, then stopped short, caught by surprise as he saw Clayton Daigle before the shelflike counter talking to the store's proprietor.

Neither saw him and he moved on, frowning. There were qualities about Daigle which aroused Powell's instinctive dislike. The big man was too ostentatious in his role of gentleman, too careful to cover the contempt for others that brightened his black eyes above his toothy smile.

He was waiting in Dexter Springs, supposedly to buy cattle, yearlings and the she-stock which he meant to drive northward onto the Indian lands which were being opened up. If this were true Daigle should normally have approached the Powells, since all the cattle which came into Dexter Springs would probably pass through their stockyards.

But instead, the man had chosen to associate himself with the grangers, with the farmers who were doing everything in their power to keep the Texas cattle from driving into Dexter Springs.

Bruce Powell was still frowning as he crossed the lobby and entered the hotel dining room. John Kleban had spared no expense in building his hotel, and the long room made its pretense of grandeur with its metal wainscoting and its swinging ceiling lamps. But it was not the room decorations which brought the quick smile of appreciation to Powell's lips. It was the sight of the girl who came through the kitchen door.

This was the first time he had seen Jenny Paraine without a hat, and the effect on him was physical. He stopped for a moment to examine her across the length of the room. She wore a dress of gray silk, cut in almost severe lines, and a small tea apron was tied about her waist. Her hair looked golden under the light from the side windows, and her gray eyes were wide-spaced, warm and candid, yet without a trace of boldness.

She was as out of place in this raw hotel as an emerald mounted in a pewter setting. He had seen living rooms in the Old South in which she would have fitted perfectly, dominating them with a natural effortless grace.

He stood inside the entrance, unnoticed for a moment, and watched the deft competence with which she directed the waitresses who were clearing the tables. Then he threaded his way across the nearly empty room, the smile gone from his strong lips, but lingering in his dark, watchful eyes.

She turned and saw him, and her face showed quick pleasure. "Why, Major. I thought you were still in bed. The doctor said last night that . . ."

Powell's slow grin was self-mocking. "If Horndyke had had his way I'd have stayed in bed all season. Am I too late for lunch?"

She drew out a chair at the table closest to the kitchen door. "I can give you a sandwich if you like. I'm afraid everything else is gone."

"Business must be good. A sandwich will be fine. Won't you sit down and have something with me?"

"I've eaten, but I'll sit down for a minute." She took the chair opposite him and relayed his order to one of the girls. When the girl had gone she said, "I haven't had a chance to thank you for what you did the other night on the train."

Bruce Powell gave her a wry smile. "There's no need for thanks. If I had used my head instead of charging into the aisle like a wild bull I might have stopped them. Have you heard anything about your boy?"

"Nothing," she said. "The man who planned that holdup makes few mistakes." There was deep bitterness in her soft voice.

Powell looked at her, startled. "You know who it was?"
"I know."

He leaned forward. "Tell me. We might get the boy back before he is hurt."

She shook her head slowly. "He won't be harmed—not in the sense you mean—and I'm not going to tell you. You've had enough trouble because of me as it is."

"But . . ."

She reached across the table and laid one of her hands over his. "Thank you," she said quietly. "I know you're trying to help, and I need help. But there are complications which you don't understand, complications which I don't want to explain."

She saw the puzzled look grow in his eyes and her grip on his hand tightened. "I'd like to tell you all about it. I'd like to ask your help, but I've decided that it isn't fair."

He said steadily, "But in a way you did ask my help when you put that reward notice in the newspaper. What if someone came in to claim the reward?"

She shook her head and her eyes shadowed. "They won't. I did that on impulse, a crazy impulse which I regretted as soon as I saw it in print. But that reminds me. Your printer wouldn't let me pay for the space. If you tell me how much it is . . ."

He was suddenly unaccountably angry and his tone was short. "That's between you and Cappy. I have very little to do with the paper. Cappy runs the *Enterprise* in his own way."

He saw relief in her quick smile and guessed that she was glad to change the subject. "Your printer seems to be quite a character. Tell me about him."

Powell still felt angry with her. "There's not much to tell." His mouth quirked in a hard smile. "Don't get any ideas about Cappy. He claims to have had five wives already."

Jenny Paraine heard the anger in Powell's voice, but she refused to quarrel.

Instead she smiled. "Do you believe it—that he had five wives?"

In spite of himself Bruce Powell was forced to laugh. "It's hard to know about Cappy," he admitted. "He claims so many things, but every time I think I've caught him in a lie, he proves to have been telling the truth. Frankly, I don't know much more about him than I knew on the first night we met."

Jenny Paraine laughed outright. But there was a little forced sound behind the laughter and Bruce Powell guessed suddenly that she was purposely steering him away from talking about the missing boy. His annoyance with her died. He heard her say, "Cappy told me about your meeting, a thoroughly preposterous story, something about you winning him in a poker game."

"Preposterous, but true." Powell was watching her face as he spoke. "I had no idea that Cappy was included in the stakes when I sat down in that game. There was a printer at the table, a man who had toted the press and type from Illinois, and, I might remark, a thoroughly bad poker player. Otherwise I wouldn't have beaten him."

Jenny Paraine looked across the table and doubted the words. She saw the square jaw, the keen eyes and the way he masked his inner thoughts, even now. "I'm not certain I'd want to play poker with you," she said. "But go on, finish the story."

Powell's smile was self-deprecating. "There's not really much to tell. The cards ran my way. The printer ran out of money. He finally told us about the press and the type. He tried to make them sound valuable, but the other players at the table weren't interested. However, I always figure that a man has a right to try to win his money back so I staked him a thousand dollars against the press, the type, the team and wagon and everything in it. When I went out to look at what I'd won I found Cappy asleep under the tarpaulin."

"And then?" she prompted "That certainly isn't the end of the story?"

"There is no end," he told her in amused self-mockery. "I'm a cattle buyer, not a newspaper publisher. I tried to find someone to buy the press and failed. In desperation I told Cappy he could have it, but I also let him know that I was moving to Dexter Springs. When I arrived here three months ago Cappy and the press were waiting for me. It's like a millstone around my neck. I can't get rid of that press. Cappy wangled money out of me to build the *Enterprise* building. I thought it was a loan until he put out the first issue of the paper and I found my name on it listed as publisher."

She was now genuinely amused. "It looks as if he has you thoroughly caught."

"I'm caught," he said gloomily. "It's worse than being involved with a woman. I finally suggested that we throw the press and type into the river, and Cappy was insulted. He gave me quite a lecture, all about it being my duty to bring the news into Dexter Springs. I told him that he could be the publisher, but he insisted that a newspaper publisher had to be a man of importance. Finally I stopped arguing from sheer exhaustion. He prints the paper every week. Every week it loses money. And because I'm listed as publisher, the bills come to me. It's a comfortable arrangement for Cappy, at least until I run out of money."

He was entirely serious now, voicing something to this girl which he had never said directly to anyone else.

"This is my town," he said. "I've helped build it so far, and mean to help more. It's all I have. It's a new home. The war completely uprooted me. Texas isn't the same and I have no family or ties to take me back. I'm here and I want to make Dexter Springs into the best community that I can. But there are forces which are trying to tear the town apart. There is organized resistance to the trail herds coming here. I'm trying to use the newspaper to break up that resistance."

She frowned. "You hear gossip in a place of this kind. I

understand that there is a good possibility that the trail herds will not come into the Springs."

He nodded and his voice tightened grimly. "It's more than a possibility. Que Layton is doing everything in his power to keep them out."

"And who is Layton?"

Bruce Powell considered carefully before he answered. "Layton," he said shortly, "is a power-struck devil who will not hesitate to make use of anything or anyone to further his own ends. Before the war he rode in some of John Brown's raids. During the conflict he was a leader in the border warfare and after the conflict he led a jayhawker band which preyed on the herds which were driven into Missouri from Texas. I met him there first, four years ago. I should have killed him then."

Jenny Paraine stared at the man across the table, seeing him in a new light, hearing the smothered hatred in his carefully controlled tone.

"I'm not trying to pry," she said, "but I simply don't understand everything I've heard. Men keep talking about the quarantine line. They say that the grangers are trying to have it moved westward to the state border and that you are fighting them. What is the quarantine? Why is it necessary? Why are the grangers trying to have it moved?"

Bruce Powell considered for a moment in silence as if trying to choose the proper words. "Texas cattle," he told her, "are infected with ticks. These ticks fall from a trail herd and if they bite any local stock that stock usually dies. But the Texas steers have built up an immunity over the years and are not themselves attacked by the fever."

"But the quarantine line?"

"I'm coming to that. Directly after the War Between the States when we Texans began to drive northward, very little was known about the fever. We drove into Missouri and eastern Kansas and the local cattle became infested and died. Naturally the farmers who owned the stock agitated against the trail herds."

"You can't blame them."

"I'm not blaming them," he said. "In their place I would have done exactly the same thing. They brought pressure on the legislatures of both states, and the Kansas legislature set up a quarantine over the eastern third of the state. That and the advancing railroad are why the drives turned westward, but as each new section of the state was reached by the railroad, new settlers poured in, filling up the vacant land, and as soon as any section was settled they began to agitate against the trail herds.

"The quarantine line has been moved westward three times now, and the last legislature finally set up this western end of the state as a kind of corridor through which the herds could reach the railroad or drive northward to stock the newly opened Indian lands between here and Canada."

She looked puzzled. "But if this section has been set up as a corridor, I don't see why the farmers are protesting now. Why didn't they protest when the decision was first made?"

He shook his head. "Because when the corridor was first set up this part of the state was almost empty. It was only last season that the railroad was built through Dexter Springs, but already the railroad land agents have filled this strip with settlers from the East. They are new, they have few if any cattle, and therefore the trail herds will do them almost no harm. If it were not for Que Layton there would be little trouble.

"But Layton is a born troublemaker. He and his family were finally driven out of Missouri and they came here. Layton sees a chance to make himself the leader of these new arrivals. He wants power, but even more, he hates Southerners in general and Texans in particular. There's no use arguing with him. I've tried. My brother Henry told me from the first that we would have to fight. I tried to avoid a fight. I might have succeeded in spite of Que Layton but for the presence of another man in town—a man named Clayton Daigle."

Had he been watching the girl, Bruce Powell would not have missed her start of surprise, but his eyes were on his strong hands which were twisting the knife back and forth as he spoke. And he missed the little breathless catch in her voice as she asked:

"What has this man Daigle to do with the farmers—with the quarantine line?"

He looked up then, but she had herself under control and met his eyes steadily.

"You tell me that," he said. "I've been asking myself the same question for almost three months. What is Daigle after? From his actions he almost seems to be promoting a battle between the farmers and the men who are bringing in the trail herds. Yet it doesn't make sense. I hardly know Daigle, but from what I've seen I judge him to be utterly ruthless if it means a hope of gain for him."

As he spoke the door from the street opened. Bruce Powell turned his head and stiffened. Clayton Daigle was standing just inside the room. For an instant he had the feeling that Daigle must have known that they were talking about him. Then Powell dismissed the thought. Daigle could not have heard their words. Yet Daigle was moving directly toward their table, a half-mocking smile on his good-looking face.

He was only a year or two older than Powell, and in some respects they resembled each other. They were both of a height, being over six feet, both were dark but here the resemblance ended. Daigle's face was heavier, more pouchy, and the eyes were heavy-lidded and mocking.

Powell thought that the man was coming to speak to him. Not until Daigle had almost reached the table did he realize that it was Jenny Paraine who had brought him into the dining room.

She drew her breath quickly and when Powell glanced toward her he was startled to find that her face was dead white. She rose, almost like a sleepwalker, without animation of any kind, and when she spoke her voice was a smothered sound.

"I didn't know you were in town. I didn't think you'd dare show your face here."

Daigle laughed. There was always an air of falseness about his gaiety and it was very noticeable now. "I seldom do what people expect me to do, Jenny. Right now it's very important that you talk to me alone."

The girl hesitated, but she did not glance at Powell. He sat there, half expecting that she would appeal to him for help. He knew from her manner that she was afraid of this man. But no appeal came. She did not even glance in his direction. Instead, after a momentary pause, she turned and, nodding for Daigle to follow, disappeared through the door into the kitchen.

The major sat where he was, uncertain and half angry, his mind busy with a dozen conflicting thoughts. One thing was obvious. For all that Jenny Paraine was afraid of Clayton Daigle, those two had known each other intimately at some time in the past. That much was plain from both

27

their manners, and the thought sent a stab of jealousy through Powell. His impulse was to rise and walk to the kitchen door, to hear what was being said. He crowded the impulse down with an effort. Instead he rose and, turning, left the dining room.

6.

THE AFTERNOON train was in and Bruce Powell paused on the hotel gallery to watch Glen Keith herding the newly arrived settlers up the muddy street.

There were only some twenty today, following the land agent like so many sheep. Yet Powell knew that for all their sheeplike actions the settlers were individuals, each brought westward by his dream of a new land, a new opportunity.

Each week they poured from the crowded East, forced on by the same restlessness which had led Powell and his brother to ride up the trail from Texas. It was all part of the same great movement, a wave of migration set off in the war-weary nation by the need for new hope and new wealth to replace that which had been destroyed during the years of bitter struggle.

They passed the hotel porch, continuing on toward the grange hall where Keith had his office. Powell moved in the opposite direction along the muddy sidewalk toward the print shop.

Every settler who arrived was a new recruit for Que Layton, an increasing danger to the shaky peace which Powell had been fighting to maintain.

He entered the print shop, his face expressing his concern, and paused to watch Ayers. Cappy was cleaning the press. He kept the cumbersome machine painted and oiled and glistening with all the loving care that a pagan priest might lavish on some heathen god.

The printer put down his rag and came to lean against the high counter and fill a spacious cheek with fine-cut. He dusted the spilled tobacco almost daintily from his dirty apron and returned the battered pouch to his pocket.

"For a man who's been palavering with a pretty woman," Cappy said, "you certainly look out of sorts."

Powell did not tell the printer of Daigle's visit to the hotel dining room. That, he felt, was Jenny Paraine's affair. Instead, he said, "I've been watching Glen Keith bring his daily crop of settlers up from the station."

Cappy Ayers moved his massive shoulders. "You worry too much. Henry rode in from the south half an hour ago. I told him you were at the hotel, sparking a new woman, but he said he was too trail-dirty to show up before a female. He's waiting for you in the office."

Powell nodded and turned out of the shop to climb the stairs which led to their offices above Len Milliard's store. He had not seen his brother for three weeks and he was eager as a child to get Henry's report on the north-moving herds.

He burst open the door to find his brother seated rocked back in the chair behind the desk, his wide hat balanced on the rear of his red head, his muddy boots hooked in one of the pulled-out lower drawers, his green eyes examining the scrawled tally sheets in his big, freckled hands.

He was tousled and sweat-stained and his face under the stubble of his beard looked drawn and weathered. "With you in a minute." He went on adding the figures on the sheets, his lips moving as he made the mental addition.

Bruce walked across to the old desk and picked up the silver-handled hunting knife which he used for a paper-weight. He stood idly fingering the wicked blade, twisting it back and forth in his strong fingers.

The knife had been one of his earliest possessions, the beaten handle the work of one of the Mexican riders on his father's Texas ranch. He ran the ball of his thumb over the deeply cut initials which he had scratched in the handle as a boy, recalling how he had thrown the balanced weapon skillfully in other days, and wondering if he could still throw it as well. He had the impulse to hurl it against the opposite wall. Instead he replaced it on the desk and looked impatiently at Henry.

There was almost no resemblance between them. Henry's skin was fair, the rose-colored sunburn which so many red-heads have. His eyes were green and squinted a little from much riding against the sun. He was older than Bruce, but there was a streak of wild recklessness deep in him which

29

kept him in almost constant trouble of one kind or another.

Had he been of a sullen nature his friends might not have been so ready to forgive his carelessness, but he was one of the most likable people in the world, always ready to help anyone, always ready to laugh at almost every joke.

He looked up at his brother now, folding the scribbled sheets and tossing them to the desk top. "Way I figure it," he said in his unhurried drawl, "there's a hundred thousand head of cattle on the trail coming this way and more to follow. I went south of the Red and talked to the trail bosses, singing the praises of Dexter Springs."

He grinned, relishing his own joke. "Daisy Honeychild would never recognize any of her girls from the descriptions I gave those *vaqueros,* and I made Frenchy Armaud's dive sound like the greatest *bistro* this side of Chicago. They're panting to reach the Springs, lap up the liquor, spend their wages at the gambling tables and go to bed with a woman."

He stretched and yawned. "I've been in the saddle twenty-two days without a bath. A man's muscles can stand just so much, and his belly can stand less. I smell like a steer and I'm dry as a porpoise that's never seen the ocean—which is a situation I intend to remedy as soon as I hear about your trip. How did you make out with our eastern friends?"

"Well enough." The major moved about restlessly as he talked. "The beef prices are holding in Chicago, but they're a little weaker in Kansas City; not enough to hurt us. The banking credits are all arranged and the railroad has promised us cars by the first, with more to follow. We can only hope that their promise holds."

Henry leaned back again, his chair creaking under his weight, and his eyes danced a little. "Speaking of trains, what's this I hear about a holdup with you playing the hero?"

Bruce Powell looked annoyed. "Who told you?"

"Cappy, of course. He said they stole a boy from a good-looking woman, and every man in town has been making his play for her, but you have the inside track."

Dull red came up under the heavy tan on the major's cheeks. "I'm going to shove Cappy's teeth down his throat," he promised. "I've spoken to the girl twice."

Henry was watching him with growing enjoyment. It was seldom he had the major off balance and he made the most of it.

"You're blushing like a schoolgirl. Who is she? I'll have

to meet her. I've never seen you color up at mention of a woman before."

The major strove to down his irritation. "Stop playing the fool. She's a nice person. Aside from that I know absolutely nothing about her. She is a stranger—at least, she's a stranger to everyone save Clayton Daigle."

At mention of Daigle's name all the good humor faded from Henry's eyes, leaving them cold and alert and bleak. "She's a friend of Daigle's?"

Bruce Powell was thinking about the meeting he had witnessed in the dining room. "I wouldn't say she was his friend. She acted more as if she were afraid of him. But they certainly have known each other before, and know each other very well."

"Did she come here to meet him?"

Bruce Powell shook his head. "I got the impression that the opposite was true. I felt that she was shocked at finding Daigle in the Springs, that she would very much rather he was miles from here."

Henry said, thoughtfully, "Maybe you can find out from her what Daigle is doing in town. He worries me. Every place I turn I run into him. I want to know what he's up to and what he and Que Layton are cooking between them. I met Tut Jackson, Daigle's riding boss, twice on the trail— once this side of the Red, once beyond. He acted friendly, but I could tell he was sorry I'd seen him. He had been talking to the trail crews and I asked several of them what he was after. They either didn't know or they wouldn't tell me, but they did say he had warned them that the grangers are making trouble here and that we might not be able to ship their cattle from the Springs because of the trouble."

The major swore. "Damn Daigle."

"If we knew what he was about—if you could get this girl to tell you . . ."

"She isn't a spy." Bruce Powell sounded angry. "I wouldn't ask her that. I wouldn't ask her anything which she doesn't offer to tell me herself."

Henry looked at him, then grinned suddenly. "A man in love. I know the signs. After all, I've been in love more times than I can remember. Let me give you some advice."

"Keep your advice." Bruce sounded sulky.

Henry rose easily, with all the lithe gracefulness of a well-fed cat. "Okay, bud, but let me warn you. Before you get

31

through you'll need all the advice you can get. You may be able to cope with men, but with women you are just a babe in arms. Come on, I'll buy a drink to celebrate the fact that we both got back here unmarried and alive." He ducked the half-swing his brother took at his head and led the way down to the street.

7.

FRENCHY ARMAUD was as much a product of the railroad construction camps as were the Irish gandy dancers who laid the winding miles of steel. He had followed the expanding track westward from one work camp to the next, his saloons and gambling houses the largest in each place.

But when the construction crews forged westward from Dexter Springs, Frenchy remained, transforming his wood and canvas bar into a more substantial structure, importing an inlaid back bar, huge mirrors and crystal lamps.

"I'm here to stay," he'd once volunteered. "I've spent twenty years wandering and I'm a little tired."

He did not look tired. He was a short French-Canadian, with wide shoulders and powerful arms. His father had been a *voyageur* for the Company and Frenchy had been born in the mountains and raised among the Indians. His face was handsome in a fleshy way, marred only by a knife-thin scar which formed a crescent, connecting the end of his right eyebrow with the corner of his tight-lipped mouth. He stood in the entrance of his saloon, one block south of the railroad tracks, and watched Bruce and Henry Powell come toward him.

"I've been worried about you, Major. They said you were sick."

Bruce Powell shook hands. "Horndyke should have told you that he was keeping me doped."

"Horndyke did." The saloon man turned and led them into the big room. "But the good doctor isn't always himself."

Henry laughed. "When he gets his skin full he thinks

he's a pink rattlesnake." They bellied up to the long bar and Frenchy went around the end of the counter to serve them.

The room was clean, the sawdust on the floor fresh, and there was almost none of the stale liquor smell which permeated the other saloons. Frenchy was a lover of fresh air and a long narrow window ran the full length of the wall above the back bar, hinged at the bottom, falling inward on small lengths of chain so that it emptied the room on the same principle as a well-built chimney.

Frenchy set a bottle and three glasses on the bar and leaned forward, talking around his half-smoked cigar. "The town has been quiet without you, Henry. Quiet and waiting."

Henry lifted the bottle and poured his drink and raised the small glass without waiting for his companions. "The first in days." He savored the whiskey carefully as it went down, and sighed, his wide mouth quirking. "It's dry work, riding in the rain." He refilled the shot glass.

"That rain will probably be our last big one," the saloon man said. "This part doesn't get the moisture they have in the eastern end of the state. Another month and we'll be swearing at the dust. I hope you both had successful trips."

"There's plenty of cattle on the trail." Henry poured a third drink and pushed the bottle toward his brother who refused. "The rivers are up and those cattle may have to swim like sea lions to get here. And after they get here what are Que Layton and his damn jayhawkers going to do? Do we have to fight to bring the cattle to the stock pens?"

Frenchy's mustache was long and black and waxed. He twisted at one end with a hand which looked white and soft, but was in reality powerful. "Layton is bad," he said, "and his sons are worse. One of them rode for a while with that Missouri gang. He killed two men. The old man is supposed to have been something of a killer himself, but he is after power with the farmers rather than loot."

Henry glanced at his silent brother with a trace of malice. "The major thinks we can do business with them. He thinks maybe they will listen to reason. He doesn't want to fight. He says there was too much killing in the war."

Frenchy Armaud's black eyes studied first one brother, then the other. "You might do business with Layton," he said quietly, "except for two things. In the first place Layton hates you. You are Texans and Southerners. He rode with John Brown in the border troubles before the war. Still, he might even do business with you in spite of his feeling against Confederates—but Clayton Daigle is paying him not to."

At mention of Daigle's name Henry stiffened. He started to speak, then glanced around the room with unaccustomed caution. It was the middle of the afternoon and the big room was almost deserted. Five men played cards at one of the rear tables, paying no heed to the little group at the end of the bar. A single bartender lounged at the other end of the long counter and the swamper had just emptied the ashes from the potbellied stove and was disappearing through the rear door.

Even then Henry dropped his voice so that Armaud had to lean even closer to hear him say, "I'm glad you brought up Daigle's name. A man in your profession often hears things that other men do not. What's Daigle after? Who is he? Why should he, a cattleman, be stirring up Que Layton and the grangers against the Texas herds?"

Armaud put up a hand to twist his cigar thoughtfully backward and forward between his lips. The diamond on the small finger of the hand caught the sunray from the high window and sent its blue splinters of refracted light across the room. His voice was low as he answered.

"As you say, a man in my profession learns much. Men talk across a bar when they would not open their lips in ordinary circumstances. How far south is the closest herd?"

"They hadn't crossed the river when I passed them yesterday morning, but they should be across by now. I'd say they are almost into the Sand Hills."

Armaud seemed to be talking to himself, thinking aloud. "It will take them several days to come in. Still, our time is very short. Perhaps I should have spoken, but I was not sure. I am now. I know what Daigle wants, what he plans and what he, with the help of Que Layton, intends to do."

Both brothers watched him with silent attention.

"It's a big plan," Frenchy said. "When you put it into words it sounds almost crazy. Maybe it is crazy. Maybe Daigle is out of his mind—but he is planning to steal those trail herds."

"Steal them?" Henry's jaw dropped. "You mean he is going to steal better than a hundred thousand head of cattle? That's impossible."

The saloon man nodded. "Of course it is. I don't mean that he will steal them in the ordinary way. Daigle is not

34

an ordinary person. I knew him in Ellsworth. He was running a lease in the Nations for an eastern syndicate. He's got money behind him, big money, and he's out to build a cattle empire, one of the biggest in the West."

"But where?"

"On the Platte to the north. He's gotten control of the north bank of the river for almost a hundred miles."

"That's Indian country." It was the major who spoke.

The Frenchman smiled. "I know that country. I was born not too far west of there. I have cousins in the trading posts who hear things. Daigle has a crew here in town, eighteen men. He has another crew farther north and a third at what will be his home ranch."

"But . . ."

Frenchy held up both hands. "Wait, please. You brought herds up the trail. You know how hard the work is, how tired and discouraged you grow. Now supposing a bunch of farmers had tried to stop you south of Dodge, claiming that they wouldn't let you come farther because your cattle carried ticks. What would you have done?"

The major said quietly, "That happened to us when we drove into Missouri. Layton was there with a bunch of jayhawkers. We fought, and we came through."

"And lost about half your cattle."

"We lost some."

The Frenchman smiled. "But supposing a man named Tut Jackson had ridden into your camp when you were seventy miles south of the railroad. Supposing he had told you about the jayhawkers, and warned you that you would never make the railroad?"

"We'd still have fought. We couldn't have driven back to Texas."

"I know." Armaud's voice raised a little. "But what if Jackson had offered to buy your herd, then and there, for say, half price?"

They stared at each other in heavy silence. Bruce Powell said slowly, "So that's it. So that's the plan."

"And a good plan," said Frenchy Armaud. "I have an idea that most of the trail bosses will sell. Most of them are like you, Major. They're great fighters, but they're tired of war. They'll sell, and Daigle will stock his range at very little cost."

Henry swore. "But what does Daigle do with the cattle he buys? He can't drive through here. Que Layton has so aroused the farmers with his lies and his half-truths that they wouldn't let anyone drive a Texas steer into the country."

"That's right," Armaud said. "Daigle doesn't. He swings the herds westward toward the state line. Tut Jackson and the crew carry it north a ways where they meet the second crew and turn the animals over to them. Then they come back south, waiting for the next herd that comes up the trail."

"If you're right," the major said.

"I'm right," Armaud assured him. "A lot has happened in the three weeks you've been away. Daigle will get his stock cheaply. The farmers will keep Texas cattle out of this country. But the town will starve to death, and you and I and every man who has invested here will lose. It will be two years before the settlers can support Dexter Springs. Without the wages from the cattle herds we'll have to shut our doors."

"If we let them get away with it," said Henry. "The law is on our side. The law set the quarantine line east of here."

"What law?" said Frenchy Armaud. "Do you think Deacon Sandson can bring those herds in alone?"

"We can get him help." Henry was beginning to sound excited.

"That," said the saloon man, "is the point I am trying to make. We have to bring in help, but that is one thing you boys will have to manage without me. You will need the merchants behind you, and the respectable people of the town. The men who own the stores along State Street and Kansas Avenue distrust me. Their wives would object if they so much as entered this place.

"But you can organize them. You have invested every dollar you own in the new stockyards. If the herds never come, you are ruined. The merchants know that—and they will help, if you can make them understand that unless the herds are shipped from here there will be no town.

"They'll quibble, of course, but there is no other way. You have to beat Daigle and Layton at their own game, and you have no time to lose. There is a farmers' meeting at the Grange Hall tonight and I have an idea that the farmers will be riding south within a day or two. You'll have to act fast if you mean to act at all."

Still they did not answer him.

"And we'll have to send word down the trail," Frenchy went on. "We'll have to promise the trail drivers that help is on its way, and if they will come through that we will see nothing happens to them."

"We don't need to send word," Henry told him. "I promised them help already. I said that if anyone tried to prevent them coming into town we'd send men to drive the animals in ourselves."

Bruce Powell swung to look at his brother. "You promised that—without even consulting me?"

Henry nodded. "I had to, Bruce. After the trouble they had south of Dodge last year a lot of the men were jumpy. Tut Jackson had filled them full of stories about the grangers, and some of them remembered Que Layton from the Missouri border raids. I said we'd send a shooting crew into the Sand Hills and see them safely to the railroad."

"Then we're committed." Bruce Powell said it slowly. This was exactly what he had been striving to avoid—an open break with the farmers, real warfare with Que Layton.

Henry knew how he felt. Henry put a hand on his brother's shoulder and for once there was no hidden laughter in his green eyes. "This is it," he said. "This will make or break us, and it will make or break Dexter Springs."

8.

COMING BACK to the print shop from his early supper, Cappy Ayers found Bruce Powell at the boxlike desk beside the type case, again looking over the latest issue of the *Enterprise*. Cappy belched in tribute to his evening meal and paused to repack his cheek with tobacco. Then he sighed. He was a man who asked very little of this world: a place to sleep, enough tobacco and food, and a printing press to work with. The arrangement at the *Enterprise* suited him thoroughly and he lived in hourly fear that the major would sometime follow up his periodic threat and stop issuing the paper.

"How's she look?" he asked anxiously.

"A little smudged." Powell spoke without looking up.

"Bad paper," said Cappy defensively. "Next order we get will be better."

Bruce Powell tossed the paper aside. "Tell me, Cappy, what would happen if I tried to address the farmers' meeting at the grange hall tonight?"

"There'd be a hell of a fight," Cappy told him promptly. "You'd probably get killed."

"I take a lot of killing."

"Sure," said Cappy, "but you'd get a lot. Que Layton is itching for a chance to jump you. He has been ever since we came to town."

"Someone," Powell was talking more to himself than Cappy, "someone should explain what is happening to these settlers. Most of them are new to the country. Only a few have livestock of any kind. The Texas herds will cause them no trouble, but they believe everything Layton says. If they knew what kind of a man he really is . . ."

"They don't," said Cappy, "and they wouldn't believe you if you told them. Forget it, Major. You aren't going to get those cattle to the railroad by talk. You're going to have to fight."

Bruce Powell rose. He felt he was being pushed into something that was useless and yet necessary. Four years of war, and nothing had really been solved. And the fight here would solve nothing. True, they might bring in the herds, but next year the fight would be renewed, and the year after, and the year after that. As long as men herded livestock they would quarrel with the men who broke the ground, who spoiled the grass to plant their crops. The fight had gone forward since before the dawn of history.

He turned out of the shop and stopped to look up and down the street. The spring evenings were already getting longer and it was not yet dark. In the half-light he saw that the town was far busier than usual. Weary horses flanked the hitch rails on both sides of the street, and the vacant space beside the grange hall was jammed with buggies and carriages and wagons.

He turned toward the hotel along a board sidewalk that was already jammed, and as he passed them he studied the faces of the farmers. These men were solid, peaceful, in their frayed overalls and worn sheepskin coats. Little men, hard-working and faithful; not gun fighters, not troublemakers.

But they had been made restless and uneasy by Layton's warnings. Each had come a long way to claim the small patch of ground which he now held, and each would fight for its holding. In this they were dangerous; in this they could change from husbands and fathers, thinking only of their family welfare, into a howling mob, crying for the blood of those whom they considered enemies.

Bruce Powell had seen such things happen before. He knew that it would take but a spark to turn Dexter Springs and the country around it into a battlefield, bathed with blood, and he held back, still hoping that by some miracle this clash could be avoided. He reached the hotel and turned off the crowded walk to enter the long lobby.

It was empty, and he crossed quickly to the dining room, pausing just inside the door to shuck out of his brush jacket and hang it on one of the wall hooks.

Beneath the jacket he still wore the neat dark suit which he had purchased for his trip east and, except for his sunburned face, he might have been mistaken for a quiet, businesslike drummer out of Kansas City.

It was already past the peak of the supper hour and the room was only sketchily filled. Len Milliard and his wife lingered at a front table with Clayton Daigle, and this combination brought the frown back to Powell's dark eyes. Every time he turned he found Daigle. The man seemed to know everyone, to ingratiate himself wherever he turned. Daigle, he sensed, was very dangerous.

He moved past the table, barely nodding to the merchant as he pointedly ignored Daigle's smile, and approached the seat he had occupied during the noon meal.

Deacon Sandson sat at the table beside the kitchen door, and Jenny Paraine stood leaning against the wall, talking to him. They both looked up at Powell's approach. Sandson's odd, tawny eyes glowed for an instant in the yellow lamp light, then dulled as if the marshal had masked them purposely with an invisible screen.

Powell sensed the tension in the air and halted, but Jenny threw him a quick smile, edged with relief. "Come and sit down, Major. Perhaps you can put the deacon in a better humor." She turned, vanishing into the kitchen, and there was a hint of flight in her going as if she were more than glad of a chance to escape.

Powell, still uncertain, sank into the seat opposite the marshal, thinking again how very young Sandson looked. And yet, young as he was, there was a hardness, a central purpose about the man which made him doubly dangerous.

A killer, Powell thought, yet not the ordinary gunman of the frontier. Sandson let cards alone, and he had never shown the slightest interest in the sporting women who lived and worked for Daisy Honeychild and the other madams.

Sandson was a man ridden by ambition, using everything with which he came in contact to further his own advancement. He had killed, and he would kill again, but always he would be motivated by the desire to forge ahead. He was a lonely man who would never ask help, nor offer any unless it served the private purposes of his own.

He barely nodded as Powell sat down, making no effort to conceal the sharp edge of his dislike. Silently he finished his pie and then, after drinking his coffee with slow deliberation, he picked up his hat from the floor at his side and rose. He put the hat on his head, adjusted his sagging gun belt and considered Powell for a full minute.

"Someone," he said, "should break up that farmers' meeting tonight. Things are getting out of hand." He did not wait for an answer, but, turning, threaded his way between the tables and left the room.

Powell watched him thoughtfully, wondering at the warning, wondering if Sandson was trying to goad him into action. Then his attention shifted, for Clayton Daigle had risen and, with marked courtesy, was holding the coat for Mrs. Milliard. Afterwards he followed the merchant and his fat wife from the room.

Most of the other diners had finished and were already gone. Powell leaned back in his chair, nursing his thoughts until Jenny Paraine appeared, bringing his dinner.

She set the tray on the table and began to transfer its contents to the white cloth. Then, meeting his inquiring look, she said, "There's some kind of meeting at the grange hall tonight. Most of my girls come from farm families and I let them go early to attend the meeting."

He smiled. "My luck to have you for a waitress. Come sit down. I hate to eat alone."

She didn't protest. Instead she shifted the tray to another table and sat down, occupying the seat which Deacon Sandson had vacated. "Are you always late for meals?"

He said frankly, "I waited, hoping you'd have a spare minute to talk to me."

Color came up into the smooth oval of her face. "Please, Major, I've had enough of that kind of talk for one evening."

He looked at her gray eyes and made his guess. "Sandson has been bothering you?"

She nodded, the color deeper in her cheeks. "You rather saved things, coming in when you did."

"I'll speak to him." The major's voice had not risen, but it had gained a note of harshness which made Jenny look at him quickly. Then her hand came out in a little impulsive gesture and rested for a moment over his.

"Don't, please. He meant no harm. In fact, he paid me the compliment of asking me to marry him."

Bruce Powell was genuinely startled. "Marry . . .?"

In spite of herself Jenny dimpled a little. "You sounded shocked. Is so hard for you to imagine a man wanting to marry me?"

He was embarrassed. "Why, no." He floundered for words. "Of course not. But Sandson is not much better than an animal. He . . ."

"I'm afraid of him." Her words came with a little rush, and all mirth had disappeared from her eyes. "He's so cold, so machinelike, so certain that he is right."

Powell said, "You aren't the only one who fears the marshal. In fact, he blazed a name of fear clear across Kansas. Men have left the country merely because he frowned at them."

She shook her head slowly. "I don't mean what you think. It's not physical fear. It's deeper than that. Sandson would grind a man or woman to his will. He'd hesitate at nothing to gain his ends. Watch out for him, Major. I saw his face when you first entered the door, even before you came forward to this table. There was the look of the devil in his eyes. He doesn't like you, Major. I think he believes you are in his way."

Powell was startled. "But I hardly know the man. I've spoken to him some twenty times since he came here, but . . ."

"I'm not wrong," she said. "Be careful of him. I've known men like him before. They're dangerous when they're crossed —very, very dangerous."

Before Powell could answer, the door from the bar swung inward and Henry Powell appeared. He looked around the almost empty room; then, seeing his brother, he came toward them.

"Cappy said that I'd find you here."

Bruce Powell frowned, his eyes narrowing as he watched his brother's progress. Henry was not drunk, but he had been drinking. Bruce could tell by the careful way Henry balanced himself as he walked. But there was no hope to escape the introduction so Bruce rose.

"Jenny, this is my brother, Henry."

Henry regarded her gravely, but there was a hint of the devil's humor deep in his green eyes. "You're even prettier than Bruce said."

Bruce Powell opened his mouth to object, but closed it hastily. If Henry got going there was no telling what he would say.

The girl had flushed, then smiled. "I don't think I'd trust the judgment of anyone named Powell."

"You can trust me," Henry assured her. He pulled out a chair from the next table, reversed it and sat down across its seat, leaning his long arms on the back and resting his chin upon them.

"Pretty lady, I wonder if you would ask my brother to do me a favor?"

She smiled at him. "Why not ask for youself?"

"Because," Henry said mournfully, "he won't do it. He's younger than I, but he thinks I'm irresponsible. He tries to take care of me."

"You're drunk," said Bruce.

Henry winked at the girl. "You see what I told you. You know I'm not drunk, I know I'm not drunk, but my brother says I'm drunk."

Bruce Powell had the impulse to rise, seize Henry's collar, and throw him out of there. But he knew that was exactly what Henry would like him to do. Since they had both been able to walk they had fought periodically. At first Henry had been the larger and had won easily, but as Bruce grew, their battles became a byword on the ranch, since neither would ever cease until both were exhausted. It was almost ten years since they had fought each other, but Bruce knew by the mocking light in Henry's eyes that the older man would have welcomed a fight with him this night.

Instead, he said, "If you only came in here to annoy us you can get out."

Henry was suddenly serious. "I did come to ask a favor, but I know that you will refuse."

Bruce was suspicious. "What kind of favor?"

Jenny Paraine started to rise, but Henry put out one knobby-knuckled hand to stop her. "Don't go. It's no secret. The only one I don't want to find out about it is her old man. He wears a loaded gun, and he doesn't like me."

Bruce Powell stiffened at the words, but Jenny Paraine was watching Henry and did not see the quick displeasure in the younger brother's eyes. "I judge you are talking about a girl?"

Henry nodded. His amusement had returned. "A raving beauty, even if she is a farmer's daughter. The grangers are having a meeting tonight to curse Texas cattle, and old Que Layton rode in to make the big speech against the trail herds. It isn't Que who interests me. He can rot and be done with it. But he has a daughter named Edna. I was at the upstairs window when they drove past and she didn't see me. I've been gone three weeks and she doesn't even know that I'm back in town . . ."

"And it will be better if she doesn't find out," Bruce said. "I've warned you to keep away from her. We've got trouble enough."

Henry ignored him, going on to the girl as if his brother hadn't spoken. "So, I'd like to get a note to Edna. I can't go to the meeting myself, since Layton has threatened to shoot me on sight and I'd hate to have to kill the old fool, but Bruce can go. Bruce publishes a newspaper and a newspaper ought to cover everything that happens in town, even a meeting by those idiot grangers. So, if you would ask him to please carry my note . . ."

"I'm not going to do it," Bruce told him savagely. "If you're smart you'll go back to your room, dunk your head in cold water and then go to sleep."

"But she's such a beautiful girl." Henry was still talking to Jenny Paraine. "It would be terrible if she forgot all about me and married a clodhopping farmer."

The major pushed back his chair. His annoyance was rapidly turning to anger. "I hate to make a scene before a stranger," he told Henry coldly, "but since you have no sense I'll have to do the thinking for both of us. We've got trouble enough with the Laytons and their friends without you messing around with their daughter. She's a child. She isn't eighteen yet. You get in trouble with her and they'll hang you, and I'd be inclined to help them. Go on, go to bed."

Henry pushed himself up out of the chair sulkily, all his good humor gone, but before he could turn away from the table Jenny Paraine said surprisingly, "Write your letter, Henry. I'll see that your girl gets it."

The major was no more surprised than his brother. Henry

stared for a moment as if his clouded brain did not understand the words; then with sudden boyishness he leaned across the table and pressed his lips gently against her forehead.

"Lady, I love you." He straightened, regaining his balance with some difficulty, and pulled a folded piece of paper from his pocket. "The note's already written. I really expected the major to go soft and deliver it." He thrust it into her hand and then, as if afraid she might change her mind, he turned and moved carefully back toward the bar, letting the door slam behind him.

"Well," said Jenny Paraine, between laughter and breathlessness. "He can be as sudden as a can of powder."

"He has no sense." Bruce Powell was thoroughly angry. "Give me that note; let me tear it up before someone gets killed."

Instead, the girl thrust it into her apron pocket. "I'm sorry." She met his angry stare frankly, but there was no yielding in her gray eyes. "I promised to deliver it and I will." She rose and the major came automatically to his feet.

"Now listen . . ."

She wasn't listening. She moved to the row of hooks beside the kitchen door and took down a shawl which she draped over her shoulders. Then she turned to face him. "Major," she said in a low voice, "sometimes people have to do things of which they are not proud."

He did not understand her, and he made no effort to. "You can't go out alone."

"And why not?"

He looked at her helplessly, then said almost roughly, "Because I won't let you."

"You can't stop me."

He drew a deep breath. "No," he said slowly, "I can't stop you, but I can go with you." He turned then and led the way toward the front door, which he held open for her passage. Afterwards they moved along the slippery sidewalk in angry silence.

9.

IN THE grange hall Que Layton had already been ranting for half an hour. He was a giant, his shoulders huge, his thrashing arms too long, his hands enormous.

But he made a striking figure, his heavy face almost hidden by the bushy black beard which concealed the red, veined cheeks, and his voice matched the rest of him, rolling out to reverberate against the thin boards of the unpainted walls. He had learned his lessons early under John Brown, and the frenzy of his words carried the emotional impact of a camp-meeting evangelist.

"You don't want to fight," he bellowed, "but who is going to keep those trail herds out? If they bring their ticks into the Springs we will lose every head of cattle we own. Now is the time to protect our property, our homes. We've got to fight if we mean to survive, and I for one mean to survive. Let me hear you. We need volunteers—fifty men to ride south with me to the Sand Hills. Who will be the first?"

One of Layton's three sons leaped to his side, followed by a second. Under the spell of the big man's voice the settlers surged up behind them to sign the roll, milling about Bruce Powell as he stood watching the platform. Bitterly he knew that without this messianic leader these men could be won by reason. But there was no talking to them now. They were caught up in the frenzy of a crusade, and Frenchy Armaud was right. Layton had played his cards well. Nothing remained but to fight. If they were to save the town there was no other way.

He turned, meaning to leave the hall, and looked for Jenny Paraine. He found her finally against the far wall talking to Edna Layton.

Bruce Powell had to admit that the farm girl had beauty. Her hair was extremely dark, her eyes coal black, and they sparkled so that they brought her whole face alive. She was small, dainty in sharp contrast to her father's hugeness, swift and certain and graceful in her movements.

He had heard somewhere that she was the daughter of a

second marriage, and guessed that her looks and grace came from her dead mother. She kept house for her family at the Layton place a mile north of town. Here Que Layton and his sons had built their home, using scrap lumber salvaged from the railroad camps. It was a rambling house, crude, without central design, but it was substantial and far superior to the soddies which sheltered the newer settlers.

As he forced his way through the crowd he saw the girl whispering to Jenny Paraine, saw them turn and push toward the side entrance. He tried to follow, but Hugh Layton was closer, and the brother shouted to Edna. The girl pressed on, pretending not to hear as she slipped through the doorway.

Hugh hesitated, started after his sister, stopped and turned back to the platform. A sense of impending danger halted the major. He twisted to watch Hugh arguing with his father and brothers. Then the four of them came quickly down the steps and forced a path toward the door.

Pete Layton was the smallest of the brothers, dark and wiry and laughing. He had maimed a man in a brawl in Frenchy's place only the month before and rumor said he had killed two men in Missouri during the trouble following the war.

He hitched his gun belt as he vanished into the night, a look of pleased expectancy lighting his tight, narrow face.

Bruce Powell did not attempt to stop them. He was too good a tactician to try to face a room full of angry farmers by himself, but he had no intention of allowing the Laytons out of sight. He reached the doorway as they were crossing the street and moved down the opposite side as they turned past the hotel and walked toward the station, outlined clearly as they crossed the light from the lobby windows.

Then they merged into the shadows before Len Milliard's. He lost them for a moment, but was certain that they were headed for Quince's Livery. The livery was a wide board and batten building facing State Street halfway between the hotel and the railroad station, which Henry Powell used as a loafing place. It would be the first place the Laytons would look, and the major, knowing his brother's careless ways, cursed under his breath since the odds were that Henry would be there.

Bruce Powell stayed on his side of the street until he had passed the lighted hotel, then directly in front of his own print shop he angled across through the deep mud. By the time he gained the other sidewalk the Laytons had turned into the barn and he paused an instant to listen. Behind him the night was filled with the rising sound of departing grangers, but nothing stirred at the lower end of the street.

He ran forward to the corner of the barn doorway and peered around it cautiously. There was no lamp in the wide runway, but a lantern burned within the cluttered office and cast its glow beyond the room, throwing the Laytons into sharp relief as they spread out under the old man's driving tone.

"Hugh, watch the front. Frank, you and Pete cover the rear." They were already moving to obey, their boots scuffing along the battered boards. Que waited until they were in place, then strode toward the row of box stalls.

"All right." There was no need for him to raise his voice; his ordinary tone shook the barn. "We know you're here, Eddie. Come out."

He got no answer and his tone turned harsher. "You hear me? Come out and take your beating, Powell. I warned you. If you don't come out we'll haul you out and hang you."

It was his daughter who answered. "I'm not coming. I'm not going home again."

"You'll come." Que Layton was savage. "No girl of mine is going to lie in the hay with a thieving Johnny Reb cattle buyer."

"Just a minute." Jenny Paraine stepped from the stall and moved with steady purpose to meet Layton. "You should be ashamed of yourself, thinking your daughter would come to a place like this alone to meet a man."

She stood before the big granger, her head thrown back, challenging him and unafraid. "And you should be ashamed that your daughter is forced to meet her friends under such circumstances. If you were a proper father she would be free to bring Henry to your home."

To the watching major it seemed that Que Layton actually swelled with mounting rage. "Grab this woman, Pete! Don't let her raise the town."

Pete Layton came rushing in from the rear doorway to seize Jenny Paraine's arm. She made no effort to resist him, but it was all Bruce Powell could do to hold himself, to wait for the proper moment.

Que Layton hardly delayed until his son had Jenny's arm before he stalked toward the stall, growling as he moved, "Since you won't come out I'll drag you."

47

Henry came, his face dead white in the yellow light. He wore his gun, but made no move to draw it. He said guiltily, "I can't shoot your father, Eddie."

"You're a fool." Que Layton knocked him flat with one swipe of his massive fist. The other two sons ran in to back their father, and this was what Bruce Powell had hoped for, that they would group under his guns. He stepped side-wise into the doorway as Que Layton kicked the prostrate Henry heavily in the side.

"Get up," Layton grumbled. "Get up while I beat you."

"No," said Bruce Powell from behind them. "No beating."

They were abruptly motionless, caught unaware. Powell fought to keep his flaring anger out of his voice. "Back over against that wall, all of you."

Pete Layton twisted his head and his dark eyes gleamed in the dull light. He moved suddenly, trying to pull Jenny Paraine around so that her slight body would serve him for a shield. The gun in the major's left hand exploded and the heavy bullet broke Pete's Layton's upper arm.

Pete Layton spun away from the girl, crying out in savage pain as he clasped the shattered arm with his good hand.

The major said coldly, "Get against that wall. I'll not tell you again."

The Laytons gave back grudgingly. He ignored their glares as he spoke to Jenny. "Are you all right?" She nodded, and he added, "Look at Henry. How much is he hurt?"

She turned to obey, but Edna Layton came out of the stall in a little rush, calling Henry's name as she dropped to his side and tried to cradle his red head in her arms.

Henry stirred groggily and managed to sit up, pushing Edna away. "I'm all right. Quit it." He struggled upward to stand swaying uncertainly as if the barn floor were moving beneath his feet.

Bruce Powell wasted only a glance toward his brother, his full attention on his prisoners. "Drop your gun belts. You first, Que. Now the boys, one at a time, and be careful."

They obeyed sullenly, not breaking the silence.

"All right," he said. "Doc Horndyke is probably at Frenchy's getting his skin full. Ride down and get that arm set, then ride out. If I see you in this town again tonight I'll kill you."

Que Layton stood stubbornly. "What about Eddie?"

Bruce Powell said, "That's up to her."

48

The girl spoke from Henry's side. "I'm through with you. I'm staying in town."

But Que was not to be denied. "You ain't eighteen. The law says . . ."

Bruce Powell's anger broke into his voice. "If you paid more attention to the quarantine law there'd be no trouble in Dexter Springs. I should shoot you and have done with it. Move out while you're lucky. Move out before I change my mind."

They went slowly, cowed by the flaming temper in his eyes. He stalked after them, standing in the doorway to watch, almost hoping that they would attempt to enlist aid, that the fight would break into the open now.

But most of the grangers had already gone. The Laytons spoke to no one. They reached their tethered horses, mounted and rode back down the street past him, headed for the doctor. Not until they vanished across the railroad did Powell holster his guns; then he was surprised to find Jenny Paraine standing silently at his elbow.

"It's strange no one heard the shot," she said, "and no one came."

He looked at her, silhouetted in the lantern light, and some of his burning anger died. "A single shot doesn't mean much out here," he said and, turning, walked back to face his brother.

10.

HENRY POWELL was a man who had never taken life with any degree of seriousness. In some respects he approached brilliance. He had a quick mind and a gambler's instinct for a sure profit, and it was he who had first concluded that they might do better to remain in Kansas as cattle buyers than to ride back down the long trail to Texas after another herd.

But it was the younger brother who weighed the plans, who arranged the bank credits and worked out the deal with the distant stockyards and the railroad. Henry disliked respon-

49

sibility. He was invaluable at making friends, at jollying the trail bosses and the cowboys, but he managed to shift most decisions to Bruce's shoulders.

He waited now, ill at ease, with the half-defiant air of a small boy who has gotten into trouble after ignoring the warnings of his parents, for he was uncertain as to the future. The major knew exactly what was passing through Henry's mind, but he waited to speak until he had gathered up the Laytons' gun belts and, carrying them into the office, hung them on a harness peg.

Returning, he said a little bitterly, "You certainly spilled the grease tonight. I suppose the best thing to do is to rout out that circuit rider and have a quiet wedding."

Edna Layton looked from Bruce to Henry and back again. She was a proud girl. She sensed Henry's uncertainty, his brother's annoyance, and it filled her with doubts.

"Not tonight!" It was a little cry. "Please, not tonight. I want a little time to think. I can take care of myself." She said this last bravely, but her voice quavered at the end.

Jenny Paraine had watched without belief. She said now hurriedly, "Edna's right. Hasty weddings are a mistake. She can come to the hotel with me. I can use more help, another girl. It isn't fair to push her into anything."

Henry Powell said quickly, "You're the nicest person I've ever known." There was relief in his tone, a decision put off without a loss of face. "Come, honey, I'll walk to the hotel with you."

Bruce Powell noticed a momentary hesitation before Edna tucked her small hand in Henry's arm and moved with him toward the street. He thought: *Poor kid. She's beginning to realize that with all his charm, Henry has his weaknesses and faults.* He stood there staring after them until Jenny Paraine touched his arm.

"I could beat you," she told him. "Haven't you any feelings? That girl's proud, and Henry is scared. You'd rush them into marriage because it would be simpler for you."

He was so startled by the unexpected attack that for a moment he could not answer. Then he went after her as she moved quickly to the street. "Wait a minute. You don't understand." He was not a man to whom explanations came easily. "If you hadn't taken that note none of this would have happened."

"I know it." She walked on steadily.

He reached out and stopped her, directly in front of the

print shop. "Wait a minute. I want to talk to you. I know I may seem cold and logical, but I'm not that way naturally. When Pete put his hands on you tonight I wanted to jump him. But I had to wait, to get them all together under my guns. If I hadn't waited, if I'd moved too quickly, every gun in that barn would have been blazing. Some of us, perhaps all of us would have been killed."

"I know. I realize that."

"And you think I was trying to rush them into marriage for my convenience? I was thinking of them. This is a small town. Someone always sees everything. There will be talk. The story will grow."

"I suppose so."

"Look," he said, "I know you meant the best in the world when you delivered that note. You were being romantic, helping young love and . . ."

"You wait a minute," she said, and her voice deepened. "Since we're being so truthful I can't let you believe that. I delivered that note for a very selfish reason. My boy, Bobby, is being held at the Layton house. There is no legal way I can get him, and I want him more than I'll ever want anything else in the world."

"But how . . .?"

"How do I know where he is? Clayton Daigle told me. Clayton Daigle had him taken from the train. He came to the hotel this noon to tell me, to laugh at my silly attempts to beat him. He boasted that although Bobby is only a mile from here, I cannot hope to do anything about it.

"And he's right. I can't. But when your brother mentioned Edna Layton tonight I had a silly idea. I thought that if I did her a favor by delivering that note she might later do me a favor in return. She might even help me steal the boy."

He was too startled to speak for a moment, and she went on with deep self-bitterness. "As usual my plans didn't work. All I succeeded in doing was in making a girl leave home. It's my fault and I couldn't stand by and let you rush her into marriage when the fault was mine."

"Jenny, listen." He reached out and caught her shoulders. "I didn't understand. I don't yet, but if you'll tell me, if you'll let me help . . ."

She shuddered. "I've seen the Laytons. I almost got you killed tonight. I won't involve you again. I won't. Now, let me go."

Instead, Bruce Powell did something he had never done

51

before in his life. He pulled a woman to him and kissed her forcibly. For a moment her body was against his, her lips warm and sweet and yielding under his. Then she tore herself free and, turning, ran along the slippery sidewalk toward the hotel.

He was too shaken to follow at the instant. He started forward, calling her name, but she did not stop. She reached the hotel door and disappeared inside.

He increased his pace, not running, but walking rapidly past Milliard's store. As he reached the corner a voice came out of the blackness of the alley which separated the hotel from the store building.

"Major, wait!"

Bruce Powell stopped, recognizing the voice, and watched Deacon Sandson emerge from the shadows into the half-light from the hotel window. A surge of dislike rode up through him and it showed in the shortness of his tone. "I'm in a hurry."

"No, Major." Sandson's words were even and spaced and deadly. "You are in no hurry. Leave her alone, Major. She isn't for you. If you ever put your hands on her again, I'll kill you." He stood tensely on the walk, his upper body leaning a little forward, his hands idle at his sides, an unspoken challenge which Powell recognized.

A wicked, all-consuming desire flooded up through the major. All the repression with which he had schooled his actions threatened to sweep away, all the annoyance of the evening, all the frustration of trying to deal peaceably with the farmers; he felt that everything could be washed out in one instant. The impulse to kill Sandson was riding him, but he managed to control himself. Killing was not the way.

There was contempt in the marshal's manner. He turned, putting his back squarely to the major, as if daring Powell to draw. Then, without looking back, Sandson sauntered to the hotel and vanished through the door to the bar.

Bruce Powell was shaking. He knew that if the challenge were offered again he would accept it. Some of his rigid control was gone and it would not return. He put a hand to his forehead and found it damp with sweat. He heard a sound in the deeper alley blackness behind the point at which the marshal had stood and whirled to meet this new attack, his hand on his holstered gun.

"Who's there? Sing out!"

"Easy, Major." It was Cappy. The fat man came forward

into the edge of light. "Don't mind me." He shifted the shotgun which he carried. "I saw the Laytons leave the grange hall. I saw you follow them and I went for help." He patted the shotgun. "Then when I came out of the print shop I saw Sandson watching the livery door. He didn't try to go in there. He hung back waiting, and I had the hunch that it would pay to watch him." The fat printer sighed. "Why didn't you draw, Major? I had him covered. I'd have blown him in two if he had started to lift his gun.'

Bruce Powell looked at him for a moment. "All right, Cappy," he said, "all right," and walked down the street, leaving the fat man to stare after him.

11.

IT WAS characteristic of Clayton Daigle that he occupied the biggest room the hotel had to offer. He was a man who had always taken the best things in life for himself, with no regard for the rights or feelings of others.

He was writing letters this morning when he heard the boots move along the hall and the sharp knock on the room door, and he glanced first at the gun which hung from its belt over the back of a chair.

Then with a shrug he forgot it, calling sharply, "Come in."

Tut Jackson came in. He was a tall man, lean and hard from much riding. His face and hands were deeply burned and his eyes were blue, looking faded and whitish against the darkness of his face. His clothes still bore the mud marks from the trail and he had not shaved in two weeks. He shut the door, came across, lifted Daigle's gun belt from the chair to the bed and sat down.

"You look like the devil," Daigle told him.

Jackson smiled. Between these two was an unspoken understanding. They had been in business together for six years, Daigle furnishing the brains and the eastern money, Jackson the range knowledge. "You'd be dirty too if you'd been on the trail. The mud is hip-deep in places."

"And the cattle?"

"They're coming north slowly. First herd is almost to the Sand Hills. Another week and they'll be at the railroad."

"If we let them."

Jackson's smile broadened. "Everything going all right here?"

Daigle nodded. "That Que Layton should run for President. It's wonderful the way he can stir up the fool farmers. He's got them believing that if Texas cattle ever reach this town the whole country will die."

Jackson smiled. He was not a man who laughed out loud. "But will they fight?"

"They'll fight," said Daigle. "With Layton leading them, they'll fight. Without him they'd tuck their tails between their legs and run."

"So long as they fight," Jackson said, "I don't care who leads them. I've been clear down the trail south of the Texas border. There's a lot of cattle moving this way, more even than we need."

"And you talked to the trail drivers?"

"I did that. I told them that Dexter Springs was a fine town, but the farmers were mean as hell. I told them the grangers were trying to get the quarantine line moved westward to the state border and we cattlemen were in for trouble."

"How'd they take it?"

Tut Jackson grinned. "How would you take it if you had ten thousand cows on the trail, if you were a thousand miles from home and if you suddenly heard that a bunch of men with guns weren't going to let you through to the railroad? They were all worried as hell, even after Powell talked to them?"

"Powell?"

"The redheaded one. He was making the same trip, talking to the foremen, selling them on Dexter Springs."

Daigle leaned forward. "Did he see you?"

"Of course he saw me." Tut Jackson pulled the small sack of tobacco from his shirt and rolled a cigarette. "We kept running into each other and he kept wondering what I was doing on the trail. I could read the question in his eyes, but he didn't brace me."

"What did he do?"

"Some of the foremen asked him about the farmers, about the chances of getting their herds through. He promised that he'd send help."

"What kind of help?" Daigle rose and moved restlessly around the room.

"Gun fighters."

Daigle stopped and he and Jackson looked at each other in silence for a long moment. "Where's he going to get gun fighters?"

Tut Jackson shrugged. "Any place. There's plenty of foot-loose riders hanging around the railroad line."

"I don't believe it." Daigle was talking more to himself than to the foreman. "The way I've got the thing sized up is that the major runs the show, and I don't think the major would ever think of bringing in a bunch of killers. He's not that kind."

Again Jackson shrugged. "All I know is what Henry promised those trail drivers. Maybe he was just talking to hear himself."

Daigle pulled thoughtfully at his lower lip. "No . . ." he decided, "there must be something to it. We'll have to move faster than I intended. Send someone out to bring Que Layton in here."

"Do you think the Laytons will still fight if Powell brings in gunmen?"

"They'll fight," Daigle told him shortly. "They had a run-in with the Powells last night. Seems that the redhead was sparking the Layton girl and the old man caught them together in the livery."

Jackson whistled. "Did he kill him?"

Daigle shook his head. "He would have, I guess, but the major showed up just in time. He took the guns from the Laytons and ran them out of town."

"Shame they didn't kill each other. It would have made things simpler."

Daigle's smile was cold. "You're a bloodthirsty critter, Tut."

"Just practical," Jackson told him. "A dead man doesn't cause you very much trouble."

"There's nothing to worry about," Daigle said. "I haven't been wasting my time. I've carefully made friends with the leading merchants. Most of them think I'm a very nice fellow. The Powells may have trouble convincing them that they should move against us. But we can't take the chance of waiting to find out. The thing to do is to have Layton raise his farmers and send them south before these hired gun fighters show up. Once we have the farmers organized and in the field I don't care how many men Powell brings in. With Que Layton leading, those farmers are going to fight like demons. You get cleaned up and have something to eat and meet me back here in an hour. I'll send a man out to Layton's." He turned and moved toward the door with Jackson at his heels.

Coming down into the lobby he found Jenny Paraine alone at the high desk. Crossing to her, he raised his hat in a little mocking gesture.

"Good morning, my dear."

The girl looked up quickly, her face whitening a little. "What do you want now?"

"What I've always wanted," he told her in his silky voice. "To make you happy. I live for nothing else."

Her face did not change, but her gray eyes hardened. "Sometime, Clayton, the world will catch up with you. Sometime all the people whose lives you have destroyed will come back to haunt you."

He chuckled easily. "Are you by any chance threatening me with ghosts?"

"Ghosts," she said. "What are ghosts—images men build up in their minds. Sometime you will be alone, dying perhaps, and those images will come to your mind. I wouldn't want to be in your place then."

Something in her words touched him, shook him. He reached out, closing his powerful fingers about her arm. She made no attempt to struggle, no attempt to get away. Her very passiveness seemed to increase the rush of his anger.

"Stop the silliness. You know I don't scare easily."

"No," she said. "You're a bully, Clayton. You like to trample other people. It gives you pleasure to see them hurt. And you don't care what tragedy your actions bring. Think of what you're doing now. You're stirring up the farmers against the trail herds. You're starting a small war, all for your own ends."

He said sharply, "You've been talking to Bruce Powell."

"And to others," she told him.

"The marshal," he sneered. "A fine man, your marshal, with his yellow hair and his ready guns. An ambitious man, Jenny. I judged him when I first came here. I could have bought him then with a promise of power, but I chose Que Layton instead."

"And now that you have chosen Layton?"

His dark eyes flamed. "I'm going to be the most powerful

man in this country," he told her. "I'm going to own ranches which stretch north from here to the Canadian border."

"You always dreamed."

"This isn't a dream." The fingers on her arm tightened. "There are a hundred thousand cattle on the trail, Jenny. Before the fall snows blow those cattle will wear my brand. You'd better come back to me. I can make you a queen."

Her voice was low, yet deadly. "I wouldn't come back to you if you could give me the whole world."

His eyes narrowed and his mouth hardened. "All right," he said. "All right. But remember when you are wasting your smiles on Powell and the marshal. You are still my wife and I'll not share you with any man. I'll kill him first."

12.

CAPPY AYERS had the insatiable curiosity of the born newspaperman. Little that went on around the townsite escaped his eyes and it was he who first learned that Tut Jackson had returned from his ride south and was closeted with his employer in Daigle's hotel room.

The fat printer climbed the stairs beside Len Milliard's store building and burst into the Powell office, puffing a little from the unaccustomed exercise.

"Daigle and Jackson are making medicine," he said. "They sent a rider out to the Layton place and old Que and his boys came busting in. From the hotel they moved to the grange hall, and riders are dashing around like crazy. My guess is that they're gathering the farmers for the ride south."

"I told you," Henry Powell said to his brother as he came angrily out of the chair. "We can't wait one more minute. We may be too late now. If the first herd doesn't get through, the other ones will swing west. They won't even try to make Dexter Springs."

Bruce Powell had been standing at the window. He came across to the desk, his face tightening. "All right. We'll have to do something today."

57

"You might shoot Daigle." Cappy said it with childlike directness. "Layton's dangerous, but Daigle keeps urging him on."

Henry, who had been glaring with anger, laughed suddenly. He always found the fat man entertaining and no situation was ever so serious that the redhead failed to find humor in it somewhere. "You're a bloodthirsty varmint," he said. "Do you believe in shooting everyone who gets in your way?"

Cappy was unperturbed. "Why not? You're going to have to get rid of Daigle sooner or later. Trouble with people is they mostly wait too long. They give the other fellow the first bite."

Bruce Powell's tone was curt. "Let's stop talking nonsense. We can't simply murder Daigle because we don't like what he's trying to do. You can't shoot a man because you suspect him."

"Why not?" said Cappy. "You step on a snake, or you hunt down a wolf. If you're so willy-nilly that you won't do the killing yourself, why, I'll be glad to arrange to get rid of him for you."

Henry winked at his brother and said to the printer jeeringly, "With your shotgun, no doubt?"

Cappy spat. "I ain't a gun fighter," he admitted, sounding cheerful. "Mostly I leave guns to those who lack the brains to manage without them. But in this case I'd drop a quiet word to Deacon Sandson that Clayton Daigle is holding Jenny Paraine's boy at the Laytons'. The Deacon would take it from there. He has his eye on Jenny, and he's direct, and from all reports he's powerful efficient."

Henry stared at the printer. "What are you talking about?"

Before Cappy could answer, Bruce Powell swung to face him, his voice quiet but ominous. "How much did you hear last night?"

"Enough," said Cappy without embarrassment. "I was beside the print shop while you and Jenny talked. Then I faded around Milliard's store to cover Sandson after Jenny ran."

Henry Powell looked questioningly at his brother, at the printer and then back at the major.

Bruce Powell ignored him. He was nearer real anger than he had ever been with the fat man. "Cappy," he warned, "don't pry. Some things are not your business."

Henry said forcefully, "Will one of you please tell me what this is all about?"

"It's about nothing," said Cappy, "excape that the major is hurt because a woman didn't choose to come to him and ask for his help."

Henry said tightly, "Shall I shut him up, Bruce?"

The major shook his head. "Let him talk."

"Then what is this about the boy being at the Layton place?"

The major said slowly, "Clayton Daigle had him taken from the train. He's at the Layton place now."

"Then what are we waiting for? Let's get some men and ride out there after him."

"Not until I talk to Jenny." Bruce Powell had come to a decision. "You get hold of the mayor and Milliard and Frenchy Armaud. Have them together in an hour. If we're ever going to block Que Layton we've got to do it now." He turned and went out, shutting the door quietly behind him.

Cappy Ayers whistled softly. "I never saw him look like that. I thought he'd crawl down my throat. Me and my big mouth."

"He would have," said Henry. "You've never seen the major when he gets started. It's something to watch. It really truly is."

13.

EDNA LAYTON was straightening up the hotel kitchen when Bruce Powell paused in the open door. She turned startled by his sudden appearance; then a slow smile lighted her dark eyes and she came forward shyly.

Powell smiled in return, finding himself drawn to her unwillingly, feeling a little protective and responsible. "How does it seem to be a city girl?"

Her smile gained a trace of embarrassment, but she was too honest a person to dissemble. "It's all right, but I'm a little afraid of you."

"Of me?" Her words caught him off balance.

She nodded. "Henry's afraid of you, too. Oh, he loves you, and he knows that you are usually right, but he's said more than once how stern you can be at his mistakes. I know you have never approved of me."

Bruce Powell said a little dryly, "It seems I've become something of a martinet without realizing it. I didn't know anyone was afraid of me."

"Oh, but they are." Her tone was eager. She was very young, and without experience, but she wanted this dark, quiet man to like her, accept her. She sensed that any hope for her happiness with Henry rested more on the major's attitude than it did on Henry.

"My father's afraid of you. He says you're the only one they need worry about, but Mr. Daigle only laughs. Daigle says that by the time you make up your mind it will be too late."

She saw him frown and suddenly realized that perhaps she had said too much. "I'm sorry."

"Don't be." His smile was quick and reassuring. "I'm very glad to know what Daigle thinks. Is Miss Paraine here?"

"She's upstairs," Edna Layton told him. "I feel so very sorry for her."

Every time this girl spoke she startled him. "Sorry?"

Edna nodded. "She asked me all about Bobby last night— if the boy was happy at our place, if he was well—and after I went to bed I heard her crying. I went in, but she said there was nothing I could do to help, nothing anyone could do."

"I see."

"I don't," said Edna Layton. "I don't see how anyone can be as mean as Clayton Daigle and my father. I used to be afraid of them, but I'm not now, not after the way you made them behave last night. I hope you aren't too angry with Henry for causing all the trouble at the livery."

On impulse he took her shoulders beneath his hands. He had the momentary memory of holding Jenny Paraine thus on the preceding evening, but he made no move to kiss the girl. Instead he said in a curiously gentle tone, "Of course I'm not angry. You're much too fine for that wildcat brother of mine. I hope he doesn't cause you too much worry."

"He will," the girl said out of a deep sure instinct. "I know he's wild and thoughtless, even a little crazy almost. But he is also kind and gentle, and never, never mean."

No, Bruce Powell thought, Henry, for all his carelessness,

was never mean. He saw the way her eyes softened at mention of Henry's name, and wondered if any woman would ever feel that way about him, and doubted it. Warmth bred warmth, and Henry's easy charm had captured this lonely girl. He knew a faint rising jealousy at Henry's ability in making friends, in making people love him.

The girl's shoulders stirred under his grasp and he realized with a start that he was still holding her and let his arms drop to his sides.

"I wanted to talk to Jenny," he said, "but I won't disturb her. I wanted to ask about the boy at your father's place."

"Bobby Daigle?"

"So, he is Clayton Daigle's son?"

"Why, yes. Didn't you know? Have I said something I should have kept to myself?"

"It's all right," said a voice from the doorway, and Jenny Paraine stepped into the kitchen. It always gave Powell a shock to see her, to realize how beautiful she was.

"I should have told you before, but I was frightened. If Clayton Daigle had the power to take Bobby from the train, he might control many things in Dexter Springs. I was careful whom I talked to, and afterwards it did not seem worth while. I had caught Clayton unprepared once. I don't expect to accomplish that again."

Powell said a little stiffly, "I didn't come here out of curiosity. I came to offer you my help."

She shook her head and her voice sounded dull. "No one can help, but it's only fair for you that you understand." She turned to the girl. "Edna, run up to my room and bring my apron, please."

She waited until the girl had gone before she said, "I'm Clayton Daigle's wife."

The words shocked Powell. Somehow in all his guesses in connection with this girl he had never thought of anything so obvious. "His wife?"

She nodded. "I've known Clayton most of my life. My mother tried to keep me from marrying him. I know now she was right, but at seventeen he seemed everything any girl could want. I married him right enough, with flowers and a church wedding, a maid of honor and a hundred guests.

"And then Clayton brought me west." She shuddered as if the memory was still very painful. "To a ranch in the Nations. I was a city girl, and there wasn't another woman within a hundred miles."

61

The major did not speak. There seemed to be nothing he could say.

Jenny went on, "I suppose the trouble was partly my fault. If I'd been older . . . if I'd had more experience . . . But I found that I had never really known my husband. He was vain, ambitious, utterly selfish. As far as he was concerned I was as much his personal property as the horses in the corrals. I stood a year of it and then when I knew the baby was coming I ran away. I went home. Bobby was born there, and Clayton never even knew he had a son until last summer when he suddenly appeared at my mother's house. He stayed a week, and when he left he took Bobby with him."

Bruce Powell said in a low voice, "Someone should kill him."

She said evenly, "I've thought of it, many times. I couldn't follow at once. My mother was very sick. She died three weeks later, and the worry and grief about Bobby helped kill her. By then I did not know where Clayton was. I hired Pinkertons. They traced him to Dodge. I sold everything and came west. I planned to steal my boy back. The law said that I had deserted my husband, that I refused to live in the home if provided, that I had no right to my child."

Bruce was staring at her. "But why on earth did you come to the Springs?"

Her wan smile had a trace of self-mockery. "Because I am not very good at planning things. When I got to Dodge I learned that Clayton had left Bobby to board with a family and gone somewhere else. I saw Bobby on the street that afternoon and took him. I hurried to the station, meaning to get out of town before his loss was discovered. There were no trains east that day because of the heavy rains, but your train was standing in the station, headed west. I dared not wait. At any moment the people who were caring for Bobby might miss him. I got on your train—anything to get away —but I never thought of the telegraph. I had no idea that Clayton was in Dexter Springs. I'd never even heard of this town.

"At any rate Bobby was traced to the station. A baggageman remembered us getting aboard and the people who were boarding him wired Clayton. He sent two of the Layton boys and a couple of his own men to take Bobby from the train."

"But why . . . if the boy was legally his?"

She gave him her little twisted smile. "Clayton explained that. He said Sandson was the only law here, and Sandson did not like him, and Sandson did like pretty women—but that Sandson wouldn't dare attack the Layton ranch. He said the only way I could have the boy was to come back to him.

"He hates me for escaping him. He wants me back to break me as he would a willful horse."

"He'll never do that," said Powell. "I'll kill him first."

She laid a hand on his arm. "Please, Bruce. That won't help. I have my own plan. If I can manage to steal Bobby again I'll vanish. I'll change my name and seek some small town where Clayton can never find us."

"But, Jenny." He had never argued with a woman and he did not know how. "I'm not going to let you go. There must be some way, somehow you can have the boy and . . ."

She stopped him by putting one hand across his mouth, her slender fingers sealing his lips. "Don't say it," she pleaded. "Don't get involved in this. You're stronger than I am. You're a man, and you're free to do things which I can't. I know how you feel toward me. I'm not exactly a fool." She caught her breath, steadying herself, then said in a more even tone, "Please, Bruce, don't put it into words. This isn't easy. I didn't want it to happen, but I knew when you kissed me last night that I wasn't as strong as I thought. Help me, Bruce, help me by letting me alone."

She fled from the kitchen.

14.

THE FIVE men gathered in the rear of Milliard's store waited in uneasy silence. Each knew why they were there, each knew that the decision which they reached might affect the whole future of the town, and each nursed his small dream of what that future might mean to him.

Andrew Hyde, the mayor, was an impatient man. He kept pulling out his big hunting-case watch, snapping it open and glancing at the ornate face.

"Powell should have been here fifteen minutes ago."

"He'll come," said John Kleban. "There's one thing about Bruce Powell—he carries out his obligations."

Len Milliard sounded querulous. "Personally I don't like

63

all this wild talk, this wild guessing. I'll admit Que Layton is a brute, but I've always found Clayton Daigle trustworthy."

Everyone except the marshal looked at the storekeeper. Since entering the room Deacon Sandson had not opened his mouth. He stood slacked against the rear wall, his slight body seeming to sag under the weight of the two guns holstered at his narrow hips. He apparently heard nothing of what went on in the room, but actually he was more conscious of each meaning, of each shading in the words than anyone else. This was the moment he has waited for, the hour for which he had planned. If things went well he would walk from the store the most powerful man in Western Kansas.

And it was this alertness which made him see the Powells first. From his position he could look through the open door out and across the cluttered store. He saw them coming and straightened. The mayor, seeing the motion, turned and pulled his watch into sight again.

"It's about time." His tone was ruffled. "Other people have business, too."

"We had to argue Frenchy into coming." Bruce Powell stood aside so that Armaud and Henry who were following him could enter; then he stepped in and closed the door.

The men in the room welcomed the saloonkeeper with marked coolness and Len Milliard said in a careful tone, "Perhaps it would have been as well if he had stayed on his side of the tracks."

Armaud's slightly swarthy face showed no trace of feeling, but Henry flushed and opened his mouth for an angry answer.

Bruce Powell cut him off. "We're here," he said shortly, "because our interests are identical. We all have heavy stakes in the future of the Springs and it's not necessary that we like or approve of each other to stand together for the town's protection. Frenchy has as much interest as anyone. If this town dies he'll be ruined as we'll all be ruined."

"It's not the same," Len Miller insisted emphatically. "I'm a respectable merchant. I give standard goods and excellent values."

Henry Powell grinned. "Have you taken a drink of Frenchy's whiskey recently? But of course you haven't. Your wife would not approve."

Milliard's beefy face reddened. Bruce Powell said sharply,

"We aren't here to bicker." He glanced around speculatively, weighing each man present.

John Kleban returned his look. He was the oldest, and most of his years had been spent in nurturing his business until he owned the most expensive property in the Springs. He smiled a little now, giving tacit agreement before the mayor spoke.

The mayor was of different stripe, an opportunist who had put money into the original townsite. He was a big man, seeking political power, not too smart, used by better men for purposes of their own. He had never consciously made an enemy, and he would always go along with the strongest party while he tried also to remain friendly with the other side.

Len Milliard was the important question mark. The other merchants would follow his leadership and there could be no effective action until he agreed. So it was to Milliard that Powell spoke, playing on the man's avarice, pointing out that a dozen cowboys off the trail would spend more in a single day than twenty farmers in a year.

"We've all seen other trail towns," he said. "We know that every rider from Texas has six months' pay in his pocket after the cattle are sold, and that they leave these wages in the town before they ride away."

Milliard stirred under his words. "But you were the one who insisted that we should compromise with the farmers."

"That's right." Bruce Powell's tone showed his latent anger. "For three months I've tried to talk to Layton. I even offered to replace any local cattle that died of fever within the next six months, but Layton refuses to listen. It means nothing to him that we are west of the quarantine line, that he and the grangers have no legal right to block the herds. This morning he is sending riders all over the country, summoning his volunteers. The question to be decided is, do we sit idly by and let them ruin the town, or do we fight?"

Milliard squirmed and his indecision was painful to watch. He was not a fighting man. He had never in his life worn a gun, and he shrank from the very thought of violence. But he too had his stake in this town and he was shrewd enough to know that it could not exist on the farmer trade alone.

"You have a point," he grudgingly said, "but we must be careful to remain within the law. We must not take action as individuals but in the name of the organized community."

Powell knew what he meant. Milliard hoped that somehow

65

the herds could be brought in without antagonizing the farmers. He did not want to lose the granger trade.

John Kleban said dryly, "We're wasting time. The only thing we can do is hire men to guard the incoming herds. How much would we have to pay such a guard?"

Bruce Powell did not hesitate. "We need twenty-five men. I don't know how much it would cost."

Kleban turned to look at the marshal. "What would your guess be, Sandson?"

Deacon Sandson came away from the wall. Ever since the Powells' arrival he had stood motionless, his tawny eyes never leaving the major's face. He said now in a flat voice, "It would depend on who you get. You're hiring men to handle guns, not cattle. I'd guess at one hundred a month, horses and food furnished."

They considered, turning the figure over in their minds, balancing the total against the amount of wages which would be spent in the town. "It's a lot of money . . ." Len Milliard sounded distressed.

"We know it." Powell felt Milliard slipping away from him and spoke quickly. "For that reason my brother and I will stand one-third. I've already discussed it with Frenchy. He guarantees that the people below the tracks will pay one-third. That leaves the rest for you to raise among the merchants along State and Kansas Avenue."

But still Milliard quibbled. "I don't like it. Who's going to keep these gun fighters in hand? What's to prevent them from turning on the town and raiding it? Most of them will be little better than outlaws."

John Kleban said quietly, "You forget Sandson. He has shown himself to be a capable marshal. He represents the law, the only law we have out here."

"Why, yes." Milliard sounded suddenly pleased. "That's what I'm trying to say. Since Sandson must keep order why don't we have him do the recruiting? Why not make our action legal by having him hire these men as his deputies?"

"That's a wonderful idea." The mayor said it quickly— too quickly—and Bruce Powell glanced around the room, suspicion forming in his mind. He sensed, rather than knew, that this had been discussed before his arrival. He saw the eager glitter in Sandson's eyes and judged that the idea might well have come from the marshal himself. A power-thirsty man with twenty-five riders at his back could well control all of western Kansas.

Henry Powell guessed the same thing and opened his mouth to protest. Bruce halted him, saying calmly, "I see no objection. In some ways it's an excellent idea. I don't suppose Sandson will object if I help him find the proper men."

Deacon Sandson grinned. Things had worked out even better than he had hoped. "I'd be pleased, of course." His tone held a shading of mockery. "The major should be able to recognize fighting men even if he has long since hung up his own guns."

The slur was obvious. Henry Powell stiffened with quick anger, but his brother's hand on his arm checked him. The major ignored Sandson as he glanced at Frenchy Armaud. "Will that arrangement suit you?"

The saloonkeeper made no attempt to conceal his displeasure, but he was a practical man and he knew that any objection from him would be resented by Milliard. "We'll go along," he said shortly. "When do you want the first money?"

"Now," said Powell. "I plan to catch the noon train back to Dodge. Since Sandson is to handle the recruiting he'll have to go with me."

The attention turned to the marshal who nodded slowly. "I'll have no trouble finding men," he said. "The kind we need like to follow someone they know, at least by reputation." He spoke with no hint of boasting. In his own mind he was the most competent leader present and when he spoke to the major there was a hint of command in his tone. "I'll be at the station by train time. You should bring money with you. There's nothing like gold to persuade men to fight, and someone must arrange for horses and housing." He looked around the room as if daring anyone to question his orders; meeting Henry Powell's angry green eyes for an instant, then nodding to the mayor.

Andrew Hyde rose as if he had received orders and followed Sandson from the room. They were hardly gone before Henry burst out hotly, "I don't trust him. He's playing a game of his own."

"Never mind," said the major. "Never mind now. We have to do the best we can."

15.

FRENCHY ARMAUD turned from his safe and put the heavy sack of gold coins upon his bar. "I agree with Henry," he said. "Deacon Sandson is playing a game of his own."

"Of course." Bruce Powell picked up the money, stowing it into his belt. "The deacon is not a merchant or a cattle buyer or a saloon man. He came here at Hyde's request and he has been using the mayor for his purposes ever since. The question is, what does he want? I think I know. I think he wants power. If that is true he'll fight with us to save the town—because if there is no town here there can be no power."

Frenchy nodded. "You're right in that. Sandson has ambitions, but he does not like you. I watched his eyes as we entered that room. He will make you trouble if he can."

"I'll bear that in mind." The major turned to his brother. "It's up to you to arrange for horses," he said as they moved from the saloon and walked toward the station and the waiting train. "And see if the Drovers' has enough beds, although we may not stay overnight in town. We'll need a chuck wagon and cook, and you'd better send a rider down the trail to tell the riding bosses that the farmers are coming and to hold their herds until we get there."

He broke off as they stepped up onto the platform and found Sandson waiting beside the train. "All set?"

A tiny mocking light sparked in the deacon's eyes. "Everything is set," he said and, turning, preceded the major up the car steps.

Henry Powell watched them, a worried frown knotting his light eyebrows. He waited until the train pulled out, then left the wind-swept platform and turned uptown, pausing at the Drovers' to arrange for beds. Afterwards he moved diagonally across the street and tramped into Quince's livery barn.

Hall Quince was cleaning one of the rear stalls. He put his pitchfork aside and came forward to meet his friend.

"You want horses?" he guessed. "I've already talked to Len Milliard and Kleban."

Henry nodded.

Hall Quince took time to spit. "I'd like it better if the major was at the head of those riders instead of Sandson."

"You and me too. You heard what happened?"

"I heard," said the stableman, "and what I didn't hear I can guess. The mayor is a fool, Len Milliard is a bowl of jelly and Sandson is using them all."

"And what about the horses?"

"I'll try," said Quince. "There's not too many good horses in this part of the country, and Daigle's foreman was around an hour ago trying to buy mounts."

Henry started. "You mean, to keep me from getting them?"

Hall Quince shrugged. "Either that or for those farmers to ride. They know what you're up to, of course. It's all over town, as if it had been printed in the *Enterprise*. I'd keep off the streets if I were you. There's more grangers showing up every minute."

Cappy gave him the same warning an hour later. "There are a lot of those clodhoppers at the grange hall. I figure they'll be headed south before dark."

Henry nodded and walked to the print shop desk. "That reminds me. I've got to send a note, warning the trail bosses."

"Write it," said Cappy, "and I'll find a man to take it south."

"No," said Henry. "Today I don't trust anyone. Take it down to Frenchy. One of his own men can ride. Tell him the first herd should be somewhere beyond the Sand Hills close to Indian Wells. Tell him to give this note to Wirt Downer. I'm warning Downer to hold his herd, not to try to push further north alone."

"That's sensible." Cappy took the note and moved to the door. "And you keep off the street until I get back."

Henry sat at the desk for long moments after he had gone. Prudence told him that Cappy was right, that he was foolish to risk trouble with the grangers; but he was angry, and pride would not let him heed the whisper of caution.

He left the print shop, heading for the hotel. He gained the lobby without incident, stepping into the dining room in time to see Clayton Daigle just disappearing through the kitchen door. Henry hesitated for a fraction of a second, and then walked rapidly the length of the room, following

Daigle. Jenny Paraine was against the stove facing Daigle, her gray eyes dark with anger.

"I asked you not to come here again."

Daigle laughed. His big body almost masked Henry's view of the girl. Aside from them the kitchen was empty. "I just thought I'd give you one last chance," Daigle told her. "I'm riding out tonight. Are you certain you won't come with me?"

The girl's answer was low, but so distinct that Henry Powell had no difficulty in understanding. "I'm very certain. No matter what happens I'll never come with you."

"Even to get the boy?"

She stared at him. "Much as I despise you I still find it hard to believe that you are heartless enough to take a child along on a cattle drive."

He pretended to be hurt. "Did I say I was taking Bobby? He's comfortable where he is, and well cared for. Once I get settled at the new ranch I'll send for him, but it would be nice to have you with me." His voice turned persuasive.

"I know that I made some mistakes. We both did, Jenny. We were both young and hotheaded, but we're older now. Give me a chance to make things up to you." He put out a hand toward her, but she stepped away.

"Better leave her alone." It was Henry Powell.

Daigle spun around as if he were on a pivot, his big body leaning a little forward, his right hand trailing close to his single gun.

Henry's green eyes gleamed, and a little smile lifted one corner of his wide mouth. "Pull it, Daigle. I've wanted a crack at you for months."

Clayton Daigle was motionless and it was not fear that held him. His eyes showed his eagerness, but he was too careful a gambler to play in a game when the odds were not set in his favor. "Sorry, Powell." He had himself under full control now. "Some other time. I have more important things to do." He turned and, without looking at Jenny, stepped through the door to the alley.

Henry Powell stood looking after him, feeling let down. "I never thought he'd run." He mumbled this half aloud, but the girl heard him.

"Don't make any mistake," she said. "He wasn't afraid. It simply did not suit his purpose to stay and fight at the moment."

"Damn him." Henry's anger was growing. "He's good at

treating with women and farmers, but I'd like to get him cornered when he couldn't talk his way out."

"You never will," she said, and her voice broke a little. "No one ever corners him or beats him at anything. Clayton Daigle was born to win—some people are like that—and Daigle is one of them."

16.

HENRY POWELL spent the afternoon in his office above Len Milliard's store. Standing at the window he watched the gathering farmers crowd the ground around the grange hall. They made an odd appearance, fifty of them, with all types of horses, from heavy draft animals to an occasional mule.

Their arms were just as varied—shotguns, hunting rifles and even the heavy muskets from the battlefields of the war. He made no effort to have a close look, being content to remain at the window until at dusk he saw Que Layton emerge and stalk toward his tethered horse.

All afternoon he had watched, fearing that the Laytons might try to take Edna home before riding south. He moved to the stairs now and dropped quickly down them.

But none of the grangers showed any interest in the hotel, and the sidewalk before him was deserted since the townspeople were keeping well out of sight. He hesitated, then cut along the slatted boards to the hotel.

Here there was no sign of activity. The ordinary supper guests were missing and the lobby dark. Henry paused in the doorway and John Kleban's dry tone reached him.

"Step in out of the light."

He stepped in. The furniture made deep shadows and for the moment Henry could not find the hotelman. Then he saw Kleban peering from one of the wide windows, nursing a shotgun in his cradled arm.

He moved across to Kleban's side and they stood in silence for long dragging minutes, a silence which Kleban finally broke. "I guess the major and Sandson didn't get started soon enough."

Henry shook his head. "I guess not. I've sent a warning south. My note told the trail boss to stall the farmers as long as he could, and not to try and fight or sell to Daigle because help was on the way."

They lapsed again into uneasy silence, waiting. The whole town waited, the inhabitants holding their breaths. It was as if a plague hovered over them, keeping them hidden indoors—and then the grangers rode out.

They did not bunch or hurry as cowhands might, and there was no semblance of order, no shouts, nor cheering, nor exploding guns. They rode unwillingly, grim and stolid, unimaginative men who had been told that they must fight to protect their homes. They moved slowly, filling State Street from hitch rail to hitch rail, a sorry bunch, straggling across the railroad, passing the river and so disappearing in the darkness to the south.

Both Henry and John Kleban had been holding their breaths unconsciously. They expelled them slowly now, and moved out onto the sidewalk to watch the last of the stragglers vanish from the lower end of the street.

Around them the town came slowly alive. Lights went on, people appeared and an air of relief filled the whole long block.

Kleban stood for long seconds, then went back into the lobby, pausing to light one of the ceiling lamps before placing his shotgun behind the desk. Returning, he lit the other lamps and then sank tiredly into one of the cane-bottomed chairs.

"I suppose it's too much to hope that Que Layton will ride off a cutbank and break his fool neck."

"I suppose so," said Henry and went on into the dining room. Here the lights had not yet been lit, but a lamp burned in the kitchen and he crossed in search of Edna. He found her alone before the big stove. He came up behind her, noticing with pleasure how her warm dark hair curled up at the nape of her small neck. "What time will you be finished?"

She turned, startled, and the color rose swiftly to tint her cheeks. "Henry, you scared me."

He grinned. "What time will you be through?"

She looked confused. "I . . . I can't see you tonight."

"You can't?" Surprise stopped him for the moment. Then he said quietly, "What have I done now?"

"You . . . Why, nothing. It's Jenny. She . . ."

His green eyes darkened. "Is Jenny Paraine riding herd on you now, telling you who you can see and who you can't?"

Edna laughed, relieved. "Henry, you can be such a fool." She glanced around quickly to be certain they were not overheard, then lowered her voice. "You promise not to tell, but Jenny's leaving tonight. I have to help her."

"Leaving?" He was startled.

"Yes, leaving. Her son is out at our ranch. We're going to steal him and then Jenny's going to get the evening train east."

"Son?"

She was impatient. "Of course. Clayton Daigle's boy."

This was coming a little too fast for Henry. He said slowly, "Are you trying to tell me that Jenny is married to Clayton Daigle?"

She nodded.

"Does the major know?"

She nodded again. "Jenny told him this morning."

Henry turned this over in his mind. Jenny Paraine was the first girl he could remember the major ever showing any interest in, and Jenny was married. Not only married, but married to Clayton Daigle.

"This," he said slowly, "is bad."

"Very bad." Edna spoke in a hushed tone. "I feel so very sorry for her."

Henry realized that all his thoughts had been centered on his brother while Edna was thinking of Jenny. He pulled the girl to him suddenly and kissed her. She clung to him for a moment as if drawing from his strength. "Stop worrying. What is she going to do?"

"Steal the boy. He's out at the ranch all alone except for old Ben. We'll rent a buggy and go out there, then Jenny will take the nine o'clock train east and disappear. She doesn't want anyone to know she's going, not even Mr. Kleban."

"All right," he said. "I'll have the buggy ready for you."

This had not occurred to her. "That's wonderful. Have it in the alley behind your print shop in an hour and a half, and don't breathe a word to anyone." She stood up on tiptoe and kissed him. "You're sweet," she whispered. "You're very sweet."

An hour and a half later Henry Powell drove the rented

buggy along the alley. The whole town was very quiet as if it were exhausted by the tension which had held it all afternoon.

He glanced at his watch and then stared impatiently toward the rear door of the hotel. Finally he climbed down and walked through the litter of the alley toward the door. He had almost reached it when it opened and the two girls slipped through, carrying Jenny's heavy portmanteau between them. He stepped forward, took the bulky bag and carried it back to place in the buggy's boot. He helped them to the seat, and Jenny bent forward.

"Thank you." she whispered. "Thank you, and give your brother my good-bye."

"But I'm coming with you." Henry moved back to loosen the lead horse and swing quickly into the saddle. He kneed the animal alongside the buggy. "You didn't think I'd let you ride out there alone? Layton might have left someone at the ranch besides old Ben."

Jenny Paraine said hastily, "But I don't want you to go. There is a reason that I want no one in your family involved."

Henry understood her partly, and he grinned to himself in the darkness. "No one will know that I went with you. I'll keep back out of the way, and I'll certainly never tell the major. Drive ahead, Eddie, there isn't much time to get that train."

The farm girl unwrapped the lines from the socketed whip, chirruped the sluggish horse into motion and drove along the alley skirting State Street until she reached the end of the townsite.

Henry allowed them half a block lead before he followed. All his life he had gone to great lengths for practical jokes. Even during the war a good part of his attention had been directed toward annoying his fellow soldiers, and he grinned as he visualized the look on Clayton Daigle's handsome face when the man learned that Jenny Paraine had finally spirited Bobby away. The right and wrong of the action touched Henry lightly. He disliked Daigle and he had grown very fond of Jenny. His loyalties were simple and direct. You helped your friends and you confounded your enemies.

The buggy pulled out onto the county road and Edna applied the whip, increasing their speed until gobs of drying mud flew from the spinning wheels. The moon was just rising, as yet little more than a faint glow beyond the horizon.

Within an hour it would spread its path of silver light clear across this rolling land. But by that time Jenny Paraine should be safely aboard her train, speeding eastward.

Henry thought of the major. Maybe it was better this way. It did not shock him that his brother was interested in a married woman, but he did sense that Jenny was not the kind to have anything to do with another man as long as she was married to Clayton Daigle.

He sighed. Why did Jenny have to be married? Why couldn't Bruce have become interested in someone else? He knew that his brother was not happy and at the times he thought about it he worried.

But Henry was not a person who worried long about anything. Already the Layton farmhouse was showing off to the right, set back a good eighth of a mile from the county road at the head of its own private lane. Henry stared across the fields. He felt a dull hatred for the Laytons and everything that they possessed; everything but Edna. Why did she have to be old Que's daughter? He had been worrying about the major. Perhaps it would be better if he worried about his own affairs.

The buggy turned into the lane and he followed. Most of the house ahead was in darkness, but light filtered from a single window on the south side, and Henry wondered if the old Negro would give Edna an argument.

He halted his horse at the fence line while Edna drove the buggy directly across the yard to the house door. At least there were no dogs. Old Que hated dogs and would not have one on the place.

The buggy halted and Henry heard Edna's voice as she raised it against the night. "Ben! Ben! It's me, Edna. Show a light."

The house door opened slowly and an old Negro appeared, holding a lamp above his head.

"Your pa ain't home. They all done rode away."

"I know." Edna stepped down from the buggy. "I've come to take Bobby into town, Ben. Pa told me to fetch him."

The old Negro sounded uncertain. "Your pa didn't tell me to let him go."

"Never mind," said the girl. "What if the baby got sick, and you here all alone."

"But I ain't . . ." The old man never finished the sentence, for Clayton Daigle stepped around the corner of the

75

house. He seized Edna's arm as she turned and handed her to a man who followed him. Then he grabbed the buggy horse as Jenny tried to swing it around.

"A nice try." His laughter came through the night. "Come on, dear. You'd better get out."

Jenny Paraine jumped to the ground. "I might have known."

"Of course." He was still laughing. "You see, Jenny, I know exactly how your mind works. I knew that if you thought Bobby was unguarded you'd rush out here as soon as it was dark. Won't you ever realize that it's hopeless to fight me?"

Jenny said coldly, "And what do you think you've gained by this small comedy?"

"Why," he was still chuckling, "isn't it obvious? I've lured you out of town where the good burghers might have protected you. I can now force you to accompany me if you still refuse to go." He walked around the buggy, seeing the portmanteau in the boot. "I even guessed that you would plan to have your things packed. See how very convenient everything is?"

Edna said hotly, "You're being very silly, Clayton Daigle. As soon as I get back to town I'll . . ."

"But you aren't going back," he told her. "Your father does not approve of your associations in Dexter Springs. He asked that I bring you south with us. It is all arranged."

"Is it?" Henry Powell jumped his horse in from the fence line, driving across the yard, pulling the rifle from its boot as he came. "You've overplayed your hand, Daigle."

Clayton Daigle swung around, caught off guard. But Henry never had a chance to use his rifle. He was still fifteen feet from the buggy when the crossfire from the corners of the house hit him.

The horse was struck first, rearing upward so that it took the second bullet in its stomach, then falling backwards. Henry tried to jump clear, the rifle flying from his grasp. As he fell a heavy slug caught him directly in the side, smashing under his ribs, threatening to tear him in two.

He fell with a confused knowledge of many voices, of Daigle shouting orders, of men rushing in. Then he blacked out. He did not see Edna run forward, seize his fallen rifle, swing it with her farm-toughened arms and crash the heavy stock down over Daigle's head.

Daigle fell, and in the momentary confusion Edna pushed

76

Jenny Paraine through the open house door, slammed it behind them and dropped the bar in place.

"Get the spare guns," she snapped at the frightened Negro. He scurried to obey. The girl blew out the light. Carrying Henry's rifle, she crossed to the window, breaking the glass with the heavy barrel.

A shadow moved in the yard. She fired at it, heard a man yell, and saw a second man trying to drag Daigle toward the safety of the barn. She held her fire until they disappeared.

Old Ben came back with the guns and she called to him, "Get Bobby onto the floor out of the line of fire."

"The boy ain't in the house." The old man was shaking. "They took him to the barn. There's five of Daigle's riders out there. You can't get the boy, Miss Edna. You just ain't got no chance."

"Maybe not." She had been watching the yard as she talked and now fired suddenly. "Bring me another gun, Ben. At least we can stand them off. Hurry up, bring me that gun before I scalp you."

17.

DODGE CITY was quieter than Bruce Powell had expected. He remembered the town from other years, when it had been the center of the cattle trade, when a thousand cowboys had walked its littered streets and turned the night into a chaos of noise which made sleep impossible.

Those days were gone, and would never return. The railroad had moved westward, the great blizzard of two years before had ruined the local cattle business and the quarantine law had turned the trail herds toward the west.

But there was still life in the town, and there were still men who made their living by their guns although the Earps had moved south, Ed Masterson was dead and Bill Brooks had fled from Jordan's huge buffalo gun.

The train carrying Bruce Powell and Deacon Sandson steamed into the station at six-thirty and they moved down the long platform, nodding here and there to chance acquaintances. At the end of the worn boards Sandson turned to look at his companion.

"You might as well go on up to the cottage and get some rest, Major. I'll find the men we need and let you know when I'm ready to start back."

There was an arrogant swagger about the marshal as if he were daring Powell to object. Bruce Powell looked at him coldly.

"Deacon," he said, "I didn't call you in the Springs because I did not want anyone questioning your authority. You and I have enough on our hands fighting those grangers without quarreling between ourselves."

"Meaning?" Sandson was balancing himself backward and forward on the balls of his small feet.

"Meaning," the major told him curtly, "that I was in Dodge before you were out of knee-pants. You've got a good opinion of yourself, Deacon, which is right and proper. But don't carry it too far. I'm here to hire gun fighters. They will be under your command, but I'm going to see that we get our money's worth."

Sandson's tawny eyes glowed. The major dropped his hand to the worn stock of his gun. "Don't try it," he said in a low voice. "I'd hate to have to kill you. I need you too badly for that."

Sandson stood for a full moment as if unable to make up his mind. It was very obvious to the watching major that Sandson would have liked nothing better than to pull his gun and settle the quarrel between them then and there. Nor did the major make the mistake of thinking that the man was afraid of him. The deacon was not afraid. He hesitated only because his sharp mind told him that the time for a showdown had not arrived. He still needed Powell just as Powell still needed him, and this need caused an uneasy truce between them.

"All right," he said, and reached for the tobacco in the pocket of his shirt. "The time will come later, Major."

"You pick the time," said Powell and started away, up the street toward Dog Kelly's Alhambra Saloon.

For an instant Deacon Sandson stood on the station platform staring after him with eyes which showed the nakedness of his hate. Then he hurried after the major, unwilling that men should think he was tagging along at the older man's heels.

They reached the big saloon which was still run by

Dodge's first mayor and turned in to find Kelly standing at the end of his own bar. The Alhambra was still one of the best saloons and dance halls in the town and Kelly was vastly proud of it.

He saw Powell as the major came through the door and a slow smile split his otherwise impassive face. "Hi."

The major came forward. "Hi, Kelly. Town looks a little dead."

Kelly flared. Dodge City never had a more enthusiastic booster than Dog Kelly. Other men might drift away to more exciting camps, but Kelly chose to remain, confident that Dodge's future was still bright, that it would some day be as great as Kansas City and Chicago.

"Just a little quiet," he said. "Wait until next year."

The major smiled. He had seen other camps blossom, and grow, and die, and he knew how Kelly felt about the town, because he had something of the same feeling for the Springs.

He signaled the bartender and looked inquiringly at Kelly. "Drink with us?"

Kelly had been watching Deacon Sandson without pleasure. For his part the deacon had barely nodded to the ex-mayor. It was very obvious to anyone that the two were not the best of friends.

"It's on the house," said Kelly, and gave his order. "What will it be, Deacon?"

"Whiskey," said Sandson, and permitted a thin smile to creep from under his weak mustache. "Neat."

They drank in silence, after the custom of the country, refilled the small glasses and drank again. Then, with a muttered word, Sandson moved toward the back of the long room. Dog Kelly watched him go, then glanced sidewise at Bruce Powell.

"Strange company you keep, Major."

"Not of my choosing." Powell's tone was short. "We're having a little trouble at the Springs."

"I heard about it," said Kelly. "Talk up and down the line is that the cattle never will reach your shipping pens."

"They'll get there," Powell told him, "if I have to carry them through the Sand Hills on my back. I never ducked yet, Dog, and I'm not ducking now. I tried my best to reason with those grangers, but there's no reason in them."

"Not with Layton there." Kelly's mouth twisted as if he did not like the taste of the name. "The man's plumb mean, Major. There's no good in him."

"Nor Daigle," Powell added. "If it wasn't for Clayton Daigle I might handle the Laytons. I'm looking for some men, Dog. Twenty—twenty-five men. They have to be able to ride, and they'd better to able to shoot. Otherwise they're dead."

Kelly did not answer at once. His eyes were on Deacon Sandson who had paused beside one of the rear tables. "What's the deacon got to do with it?"

"He's the boss." Powell made a wry face. "These men will serve as his deputies. The merchants want to keep everything legal."

"The merchants always want to keep everything legal." There was bitterness in Dog Kelly's voice. He knew exactly what Powell was up against. He had seen exactly the same situation in Dodge City—cattlemen lined up against the farmers, with the town merchants standing in the middle.

"But watch out for Sandson," he warned. "I know him. He came in here as a kid. He used to follow Bat Masterson around, trying to ape every motion Bat made. But he smartened up fast. He's not like most of the gun fighters we had here. He's ambitious and he's tricky."

"I know that."

Dog Kelly looked at the younger man. He had broken a code by saying as much as he did. A man was supposed to form his own judgments, to make his own decisions. But he liked Powell and he did not like Sandson.

"Do you want me to help you find the men you need?"

Powell nodded. "You know who is in town. I don't. I'd appreciate it if you would send out the word. I want to get the two o'clock train back west if possible. We haven't much time. In fact, we haven't any time at all."

Kelly nodded. "Go on back and take the empty table on the right. I'll send them along to you as soon as I can. They won't be beauties, that I'll promise you."

Powell grinned faintly. "For the work we have to do, we don't want beauties. We need men who fight because they like to." He turned and walked back to the table, sitting down so that his shoulders were against the wall.

Sandson saw him come and walked across the dirty floor, a little swagger in his gait. He dropped unasked into a chair and said without inflection, "Kelly going to find our men?"

"He said he'd send out the word."

"I don't like Kelly." Sandson's words were measured. "But he can save us a lot of tramping around."

Powell did not answer. He sat there waiting. The word had gone out along Front Street, into the saloons and dives, into the maze of twisting thoroughfares, even into Tin Can Alley.

The men they wanted came straggling in. Some were hopeless, some sneeringly belligerent, some pathetically eager. Powell sat back and listened as Sandson questioned each man. The questions were short and sharp and to the point. For the ones he wanted Sandson had a nod.

He bought them a drink, sometimes two or three. He said, "You'll do. Pick up your gear and meet us at the station. We're taking the two o'clock train west."

For the ones he could not use he merely shook his head. "Sorry," he said. "Go tell the bartender the drinks are on me." One or two argued; the rest shuffled away, for the ones that Sandson turned down were human wrecks, too far gone in liquor to be trustworthy with a gun.

Only once did Powell interfere, and even as he did so he wished that he had kept out of it. The man was old by the deacon's standards. He might have been fifty, or fifty-five. He still wore the buckskin of the buffalo hunter and the mountain man, and he had been around Dodge since the town was little better than a hide camp.

Dog Kelly brought him back to the table. Dog said, "This is Lefty James. He's no gunman, but he's handled himself in plenty of fights."

The deacon's tawny eyes went over James' weathered face, his blackened clothes. He said without emphasis, "Too old," and turned his head.

Powell had been watching James' face. He saw the flame of anger show in the pale, washed-out blue eyes, saw it flare and die. He saw the man's shoulders droop as he turned away. Dog Kelly had sworn under his breath. Kelly wasn't pleased and it was as much because of Kelly as anything that the major said, "Wait a minute."

They all turned to look at him. He felt Sandson's eyes, impatient, intolerant, and he ignored Sandson. "You don't look so old to me," Powell said to James.

"I can still ride." The words were unemotional. It was not in Lefty James to beg from any man.

"You'll do," said Powell. "Meet us at the station before train time." He leaned back, his eyes on Sandson.

The marshal watched the old buffalo hunter cross the crowded room and step out through the door. Then he turned

81

to say insolently, "I didn't know we were running an old people's home."

"Some day," the major told him, "you may be old yourself."

"When I am," said Sandson, "I'll own more than a rifle and a shirt of chewed buckskin."

"If you live that long." Dog Kelly still stood beside the table.

Sandson stiffened. For an instant Bruce Powell thought the marshal would come out of his chair to face Kelly. Then Sandson got hold of his temper and shrugged. "I'll live."

"That's what every gun fighter on the frontier thought." Kelly no longer troubled to hide his contempt. "I've seen them come, and I've seen boot hill fill up." He turned away from the table and went back to the bar.

18.

JENNY PARAINE had spent almost a year at Daigle's ranch in the Nations. In that time she had learned to handle a gun, but she had never before fired at a man. She stood now at one of the windows of the Layton house, peering out across the dark yard toward the barn.

She knew that if Daigle's riders attacked the house she would shoot in an effort to kill, but she did not fire on the barn. In the first place, her boy was hidden somewhere in that weathered building and she would not chance a stray bullet that might reach him. In the second, Daigle's men showed no stomach for attacking the house. Edna Layton's first shots had been too well directed for their comfort.

They had dragged Daigle around the corner of the barn and now there was no sight of them, although the moon had now risen enough to light the yard.

Henry Powell still lay where he had fallen, and Jenny was certain that he was dead. She heard Edna move across the dark room behind her and heard the girl's strained voice.

"I'm going out after Henry."

"No." The word rose impulsively in Jenny's throat, but she choked it down just in time. Of course Edna had to go after Henry. She herself would have charged the barn if she thought there was any hope of regaining her son.

"Cover me," Edna said, and moved away. But before she could reach the house door Jenny called sharply, "They're riding away!"

And they were riding away. She saw them clearly as they came out from behind the barn. One of the men carried Bobby, a small humped figure, before him on the saddle. Daigle was mounted, but a man rode at his side, steadying him as they went out through the muddy lane.

Jenny called out, but none of them paid any attention. Edna had unfastened the door and rushed across the yard, dropping on her knees at Henry's side. Jenny followed, unconsciously bringing the rifle with her.

She stopped, but her eyes were on the disappearing riders, not on the man on the ground.

"He's not dead." It was Edna, and there was a break in her voice. "He isn't dead, Jenny. Help me, help me."

Jenny Paraine dropped the rifle and bent to help the younger girl. What she saw turned her sick. The whole front of Henry's shirt was soaked with blood and his face looked thin and waxlike in the silver glow from the moon.

Someway, between them, they managed to hoist his hundred and eighty pounds into the buggy. Someway Edna managed to hold him in her arms as Jenny drove back to town. Never afterwards did she have a clear memory of that ride. It seemed utterly unreal. It was as if all this were happening to someone else, that she was an observer watching from the sidelines. She drove up before the hotel, jumped down into the ankle-deep mud, almost slipped and fell before she gained the gallery, and came bursting into the lobby, calling Kleban's name.

Kleban had been behind the high desk. He ran forward catching her arms. "Jenny! Miss Paraine, what's happened?"

"It's Henry," she panted. "He's in the buggy—shot."

John Kleban took charge. He stuck his head through the barroom door, yelling for help. Half a dozen men lifted Henry from the buggy, carried him across the lobby and up the stairs.

Horndyke, dragged from Armaud's saloon, came red-eyed and smelling of whiskey, but suddenly sober. Jenny stood in the doorway watching the doctor's deft movements, wondering about the man.

Something had driven Horndyke from his home, something had turned a competent doctor into a drunken shadow of a man. Grief seemed to have touched everyone in Dexter Springs in one way or another, and her own feeling of despair was softened by the knowledge that others had burdens too.

She looked at Edna, white-faced yet businesslike, as the girl moved about, quickly obeying the doctor's orders. She saw John Kleban standing to one side, his face expressionless. She saw Horndyke straighten and heard him say, "The bullet went clear through."

"Then he'll live?" It was Edna's voice.

The doctor shook his head. "Who knows? He's shot in the stomach, girl. That isn't good. It isn't good at all."

She saw Edna's face crumple and break like a twisting piece of cardboard. She went forward quickly and took Edna in her arms and felt the convulsive dry sobs as they shook the slight body. She could think of nothing at all to say.

Instead her thoughts were of the major. *I've brought him nothing but grief,* she thought, *nothing but grief. Everything that I do has made it harder for him.*

She turned then, forcing Edna from the room, and looking up, met John Kleban's level eyes. Then she moved past him and into Edna's room.

19.

BRUCE POWELL tried unsuccessfully to sleep as the two o'clock train jolted westward over the uneven tracks. Around him the hired crew snored in twenty different keys, the sound of their slumber blending not unpleasantly with the forward rush of the train.

At his side Sandson's slight body was slack, at ease, swaying with each motion of the creaking car. Powell looked at him, studying the marshal's relaxed face, and decided that he disliked the man more thoroughly than ever. There was a lean-jawed hungriness about the face which reminded him unpleasantly of a starving wolf, and even in sleep Sandson seemed to exude an arrogant confidence which was entirely offensive.

But he had to admit the marshal's worth. He had watched the faces of the men as Sandson talked with them, and noted the respect in their hard eyes. It was a dangerous crew with nothing to bind it together save their respect for Sandson's reputation. Without a strong hand it could well degenerate into a mob, a mob that would prey on and pillage the countryside.

He wondered then if Sandson were strong enough to hold them in check and decided that he probably was. Sandson was not the kind to brook interference from anyone, and he certainly would not hesitate to kill if it served his purpose. That was the real question. What was Sandson's purpose? What private plans was he nurturing in the dark recesses of his mind?

He yawned and stretched and the whistle shrilled. The combined motion and sound awakened the marshal. His tawny eyes came open to stare fixedly into the major's dark ones, unblinking and instantly alert, like an aroused animal.

Then he smiled, but there was no humor in the twisting of his lips—rather, a mockery, as if he had read the thoughts which were crowding through Bruce Powell's mind.

The whistle shrilled again and he twisted to peer through the dirt-stained window, noting where they were. Afterwards he was again asleep, leaving Powell to his lonely vigil. He slept easily, untroubled until the whistle shrilled again, this time blowing for the Dexter Springs station.

Again his eyes were open. He straightened, looked through the window, then back at Powell. "Almost there." He rose, stretching. Some of the other men were beginning to stir.

Sandson straightened his gun belt with a small swivel motion of his hips and looked along the car. "A fine crew." He was speaking softly, almost to himself. "As pretty a crowd of cutthroats as you will ever see together, unhung."

The major looked up in surprise and Sandson caught the look. It was like a hound showing his teeth when he smiled. "And we make a fine set of leaders, Major, hating each other as we do."

Powell nodded, and Sandson looked at him with a shade of curiosity. "I can't understand you, Major. I've watched you ever since you came to the Springs. I don't know what you're after, what you really hope to gain."

"I buy cattle," Powell said, shortly. "I only try to make certain that there will be cattle for me to buy."

"Of course." Sandson nodded. "But after that what do

you hope to gain? You could have made yourself the big man in this part of the country."

"Is that what you're trying to do?" The major was curious.

"That's what I'm going to do," Sandson said. "Don't get in my way, Major. Don't try to stop me. I'll let no man stop me."

"That depends," Powell told him, "on what you try to do. There's one thing I want understood." He glanced along the car. "These gunmen will stay in bounds. We're paying them to help bring in the cattle, not to run wild over the country. Tell them I will stand for nothing like that. Tell them that if they fail to stay in line I'd hang one of them as quickly as I'd hang Que Layton."

Sandson's eyes showed a trace of amusement. "You're like all the rest, Major. You hire men to fight for you, and you expect that once they have stopped fighting they will quickly go away. These men are almost outlaws. They are the only kind that will do us any good. They can be controlled, but they have to be controlled by force. There is nothing else that they will understand. The Laytons are breaking the law when they try to prevent those herds from reaching the railroad. I'll stop them, and I'll kill every man who gets in my way. And that, Major, includes yourself."

Bruce Powell sat very quiet for a moment. He knew that this was no idle talk; Sandson had already made up his mind that Powell must die. But it was part of the curious code under which the man operated that he felt called upon to give this warning. Bruce did not answer. There was nothing to say.

Sandson watched him a little mockingly for an instant, then turning, moved down the car, shaking the men. They came awake, taut and grumbling, made surly and ill-tempered by a lack of sleep and too much alcohol. They rose grumpily and began collecting their possessions as the train pulled into the station.

Bruce Powell suddenly found the close air of the car oppressive. Rising, he stepped out onto the open back platform and dropped down the steps before the train had ceased moving. He saw the crowd beside the yellow station building and looked for his brother, and failed to find him.

Len Milliard was standing there with John Kleban and Quince at his elbow. Bruce Powell moved over to them as the marshal came down the steps, followed by his men.

"Where's Henry?"

Kleban opened his mouth to answer, but it was Milliard who said excitedly, "He rode into a trap last night out at the Layton place. He went out there with the girl from the hotel dining room. They meant to steal that boy and . . ."

Bruce Powell reached out and caught the fat merchant by the front of his coat. "How badly is he hurt?"

It was Kleban who said in an unhurried tone, "He's bad, Bruce. Through the stomach."

"Ah," said Bruce Powell and knew a sudden sickening certainty that Henry would die. "And the girl? Was she hurt? Did they get the boy?"

"She wasn't," said John Kleban, "and they didn't get the boy." He went on, concisely telling Powell what had happened. "The Layton girl grabbed Henry's rifle," he finished. "She and Jenny forted up in the house and stood off Daigle's riders. They finally pulled out, taking Daigle and the boy with them."

The marshal shoved forward to Powell's side. His flat voice had an insistent note. "You're sure Jenny wasn't hurt?"

John Kleban hardly glanced at him. "I'm sure," he said without troubling to look at Sandson. "Henry's at the hotel, Doc Horndyke is with him."

"And the Laytons?" Sandson was still demanding attention. "Where were they when this happened?"

"Gone," said Kleban. "The farmers rode south at dark last night. That's why Jenny thought she would have a chance to take the boy."

20.

JENNY PARAINE met Powell as he ran up the stairs from the lobby. She had just come from Henry's room and her eyes were red from tears or lack of sleep. She looked at him for a long instant, then stood aside so he could enter.

Henry Powell lay unmoving on the bed, his freckles standing out in sharp contrast against the translucent waxlike skin. His breathing was labored, and Horndyke bent over him. He turned at the sound of the major's entrance and then relaxed a little.

"Don't worry about the noise. He won't hear you."

Powell moved to the edge of the bed. "You mean he's . .

"Not yet," said the doctor. He dragged a pint bottle from his hip pocket, pulled out the cork, scrubbed his neck with the palm of his hand and extended it to Powell. "Take a little of this."

Powell refused, shaking his head. Horndyke shrugged, tilted the bottle and let a third of its contents run down his big throat. "I need that. I've been with him all night." He returned the bottle to its place and wiped his bearded lips.

Powell asked automatically, "Will he make it?"

Horndyke shrugged. "Through the belly?" he said. "I can't tell. He lost a lot of blood before those two girls got him into town, and he may still be bleeding inside. The slug came out itself. At least we don't have to dig for that."

Powell looked back at the bed. They had not been much together, Henry and he. The war years had separated them. But, despite that and their difference in temperament, they had been close.

He turned away heavily, feeling the skin draw taut across his cheekbones and at the hinges of his jaw. "And no one knows where Daigle is now?"

The doctor looked at him shrewdly.

"No one knows," he said. "Edna Layton bashed his head with the rifle. The crew hauled him out with them—south, I guess. At least that's the direction the grangers went."

Bruce Powell did not answer. He stood for a long moment looking down at his brother; then he reached out, touching Henry's hand where it lay against the blankets. He turned then and stepped from the room, and found Jenny Paraine waiting for him in the hall.

She saw the tight, black look on his lean face and put out a hand as if to stop him. He took the hand, looking at her and apparently not seeing her.

"It's my fault." She said in a tone so low that it was hard to believe that he could hear. "I've brought you nothing but trouble ever since I came."

"No," he told her. "There's no need to blame yourself. The trouble here was shaping up long before you came."

"But if I hadn't gone out there last night . . . if I hadn't fallen into Daigle's trap . . . if Henry hadn't ridden in blindly to my aid . . ."

"You didn't ask him to go." It was Edna Layton, standing

a dozen feet away. She came slowly toward them, and Bruce Powell turned. It was the first time he had seen the girl since his arrival and his first thought was: *She hasn't been crying, but her eyes show how badly this hurts her.* And in thinking of her grief he lost some of his own.

"I let him go," said Edna Layton. "I told him what we meant to do. If I hadn't told him he would never have known. If I hadn't let him go with us he'd be all right now."

"He will anyway," Bruce Powell said without believing it. "Horndyke's a good doctor. I won't stop hoping until he tells me that it's no use."

She stared at him for a long moment, then swayed toward him. His long arms opened instinctively to receive her, to hold her slight body close.

Her fingers bit into his shoulders and he felt her shudder convulsively. "You mean it?" Her voice was muffled by the cloth of his coat.

"Of course," he said, and strangely found reassurance in his own words. "Of course I do. It will take more than one bullet to kill Henry. You wait and see."

And then she was crying as the tight resolve of her control broke. It was like a dam giving way, as if she had held herself in until he arrived.

"I believe you," she managed between sobs. "I've got to. I've got to."

He stooped then and, picking her up, carried her into her own room and placed her on the bed. Jenny Paraine followed him and he turned to her, his own uncertainty forgotten in his need to help someone else.

"Stay with her. I'll have Horndyke give her something to quiet her."

She looked at him. "And what are you going to do?"

He was surprised. "Why, ride south," he said slowly. "Nothing has changed. There is still a job to be done. Henry would be the last person in the world who would want me to shirk it." He turned and moved toward the hall.

21.

CAPPY AYERS found Bruce Powell in the rooms over Milliard's store where Powell had gone to change clothes. "You'd better come down," he said. "Sandson has cut loose. He's ridden out to burn the Layton Place."

Powell had just been drawing on his boots. He stood up and fastened the gun belt around his narrow hips. "Burn the Layton place? Is he crazy?"

"It depends on how you look at it," the fat printer said. "From Sandson's angle, it's a logical move. The Laytons are the leaders of the grangers, and if their house goes up in smoke it will be a warning to all the farmers that they stand to lose whatever they have. But with the deacon it goes deeper than that. It was at the Layton house that Jenny Paraine's boy was held and I suspect that in some twisted manner Sandson feels that by striking at the Laytons he will be currying favor with the girl."

Powell swore softly. "The damn fool. Doesn't he know that if he burns that ranch he's apt to solidify the farmers against us? And it puts us outside the law. Before, we were merely trying to protect the incoming herds. Now we're destroying property, and these people have been taking up government lands. He'll have a bunch of federal marshals buzzing around our ears."

"Don't tell me," said Cappy. "Tell him."

"I will." Powell reached for his brush jacket. "Get me a horse from Quince's."

"I already have," said Cappy. "There are two out in front. While I was doing it I brought one along for myself. I rather thought you'd want to take a ride."

Powell looked at the fat man, started to speak, changed his mind and led the way toward the stairs. As they mounted and rode out along State Street he was conscious that people watched them from every doorway and he thought grimly, *No matter what happens at Layton's or down the trail, the town will blame me. They will hold me responsible.*

90

But he put this behind him as he dug his spurs into the horse and drove it forward over the rutted road. He could see the Layton house long before they reached the turn into the lane, see the grouped horses of Sandson's men, and then the plume of smoke, faint at first, dissipated by the steady wind, increasing in volume until as he swung into the lane he could see flames leaping from the roof and knew that it was too late to halt the destruction.

Sandson saw them coming and walked across the yard. The barns were burning by this time and the riders grouped the loose stock toward the pole corral.

There was a swagger in the marshal's manner and a pleased half-smile lifting one corner of his thin-lipped mouth. "Well, that's a job done."

Bruce Powell's impulse was to swing down and slap the smirk from the marshal's face, but he held his heated words. It was too late to check the fire, too late to save the house or barns.

He got down slowly, looping the reins over one arm. The riders in the yard turned to look at the new arrivals and then came forward, sensing trouble, drawn by the sure instinct of their kind.

Sandson sensed it too. The lift went away from the corner of his mouth, leaving it straight and hard, but the mocking light was back in the catlike eyes.

"Maybe you don't think this is such a good idea?" he said softly.

"Maybe I don't," said Bruce Powell. From the corner of his eye he saw that the riders were forming a half-circle, facing him: that Cappy Ayers had shifted his fat body in his saddle and brought up his shotgun so the twin barrels frowned at the facing riders. "In fact, it's a damn poor one."

"Major," said Sandson, "I don't understand you at all. Your brother was shot down like a dog in this very yard. Why aren't you riding after the men who did it? Why come out here to interfere with me when I'm doing what I'm paid to do?"

"Who is paying you to burn that house?"

"Major," said Sandson, "let's get one thing straight between us. You're proud, and you've cast a long shadow in this part of the country ever since you came. But you aren't the only man here. I am hired by the town, and I take my orders from the mayor. Hyde gave me the job, and Hyde is the only man who can take it from me."

Bruce Powell let his eyes range slowly about the semicircle of watching men. Several of them were grinning; one or two had dropped hands to their guns. In a showdown between himself and Sandson there was no question with whom they would side.

Nor was it wise for him and Sandson to quarrel openly. If they meant to ride south together it was important that these hardcases did not think there was too much dissension between the leaders.

He said in a carefully controlled voice, "I'm not asking you to take my orders. I'm only saying that burning ranches and turning farmers against us is not the way. The sooner we start south the better. Whatever is between us can wait for settlement until after the herds are safe."

He mounted then and drove his horse out of the lane, conscious that Cappy rode hard at his heels, conscious that Sandson stood in the yard, grinning after them. As he reached the roadway he slowed his horse and Cappy pulled alongside.

"You're going to have to kill him," the fat man said. "There's too much between you, Major. One of you is going to have to die."

Powell glanced at the printer's red face. "There's nothing much between us, Cappy."

"Isn't there?" said the printer, and sounded a little mocking. "There's the girl, for one thing. Sandson wants her, and he knows that she favors you, and it is wormwood eating at his soul."

"Cappy!"

"Well?"

"She's married to Daigle. Sandson doesn't know it yet, but she can never mean anything to him, or to me."

The fat man considered in silence. "If Daigle were dead . . ."

"But he's not dead," Powell pointed out, "and I can't kill him. Do you see how my hands are tied? I didn't think of it before, not until you spoke, but Daigle is as safe from me as if he were sheltered in a church. I certainly couldn't go to her if her husband's blood were on my hands."

"Sandson wouldn't let a thing like that stop him. Maybe I should tell him that she's married. At least that would help take him off your neck."

"You'll tell him nothing."

Cappy shook his head mournfully. "Then I'm going to have to watch you every minute. Sandson means to get you, and in a way that you least suspect. I could see it in his eyes. He's a schemer. He has a plan. You're going to have to watch him, to watch him every minute."

22.

IT WAS after dark before Bruce Powell started south. As he rode down Kansas Avenue with Sandson at his side and the gunmen strung out behind, he knew that the townspeople breathed a sigh of relief. They feared these quiet riders as much as they feared Layton's farmers and they would not breathe easily until all sound of their passage died in the distance.

The major pulled ahead with Cappy on his right. He had tried to discourage the fat man from coming, but without success. "You're a printer," he said, "not a fighting man. You'll be more trouble than you're worth. After two days you'll be so saddle-galled that I'll have to boost you onto your horse."

Cappy had merely grunted. "You can't go alone," he pointed out. "If Henry was riding with you I wouldn't worry, but alone you are not a match for Sandson and his killers, let alone for the farmers and Daigle."

He rode, carrying his shotgun, and after an hour his groans could be heard above the creak of the saddle leather. Bruce Powell pushed forward, unheeding. He knew a certain relief to be in the saddle again, to feel the cold night air against his skin, to feel the steady jar of his horse's hoofs on the soft earth.

Their progress was slow, geared to the chuck wagon which rumbled along behind them, the canvas on its bows whipping in the ceaseless wind.

Sandson had dropped behind with the men, content for the moment to let Bruce Powell hold the place of honor as they drifted across the moonlit waste.

Cappy, who did not like prolonged silence, spoke as they

drew up near midnight to blow their horses and stretch their cramped muscles.

"I could walk faster," he complained.

Bruce Powell looked at him. "If you had your way we'd kill the horses thirty miles this side of Indian Wells. If we had a big remuda it would be different, but these horses have to last. We'll bed down before dawn, catch four hours' sleep, get some hot food and push on. The wagon can follow."

The fat man grumbled, but after the morning rest Powell was forced to shake him a dozen times before he crawled from his blankets. After breakfast the country turned steadily rougher. The men grew sour-voiced and wire-tempered, drugged by the lack of sleep and surly with the prospect of a long day in the saddle. It had turned warmer, with a soft breeze stirring up from the south, and they rode directly into it, twisting through the low-lying Sand Hills.

"Wonder how Henry is?" It was Cappy, ranging along at Powell's side. "It would be nice if he was riding with us."

Powell had consciously kept his thoughts away from Henry. The war had taught him that you worried about the immediate, the thing ahead, that you put everything else from you that was not involved with your minute-by-minute existence. That was the way it had to be. You could not divide your attention and hope to live. There was nothing you could do about things which were distant from you.

"That's Horndyke's job," he said, and sounded almost brutal in his effort to keep his voice clear of feeling. "At least Henry was conscious before we left. At least he knew that we were riding out to bring the herds through."

Cappy grunted and they pushed forward in silence. Bruce Powell had never covered this portion of the state before and he wished again that his brother was with them. The country was worsening, the hills growing larger and more barren, washed and gullied by ancient floods. It was a desolate land with little feed, brown and sandy.

Sandson had never been through the country before and at the noon halt he appealed to his men. "Anyone know exactly how the trail runs between here and Indian Wells?"

It was James, the old buffalo hunter, who stepped forward. Up until now Sandson had treated the old man with contempt, but he listened while James drew a crude map on the packed ground with a pointed stick.

"Here's Indian Wells," the hunter said, "beyond this row of hills. The hills make a kind of ridge, and it's all nasty ground. The trail follows the only decent pass and it's narrow. If I were a farmer and set up to stop a herd, I'd cover that pass." He sat back on his boot heels and watched Powell and Sandson with red-rimmed, unblinking eyes.

The marshal was studying the rough map "How far south is this ridge?"

Lefty James looked south, considering. "Maybe fifteen, maybe twenty miles. We'll hit it about dark, I guess."

"All right," Sandson turned toward his horse, "let's ride."

As they mounted, the hide hunter pushed his horse to Powell's side, and they rode forward in steady silence until James cleared his throat. "I don't like the setup. Sandson is spoiling for trouble and most of the crew are young and full of beans. They want nothing so much as a shooting match."

"So?" Bruce Powell was cautious. He could not be certain what the hunter wanted.

"So I don't like shooting." Lefty James spat between his thick black whiskers. "I've seen enough to last a lifetime."

"Maybe you shouldn't have come."

"Maybe I shouldn't." James spat again. "If you were leading I wouldn't mind. I just thought I'd let you know." He touched the horse with his spurs and the animal surged ahead, leaving Powell to stare after the hunter, a frown drawing his brows almost together.

23.

IT WAS an hour after sunset, but there was still a lingering trace of light along the western sky. The country was much worse than it had been, chopped up with gullies, made treacherous by potholes. Ahead, hardly a couple of miles, the range of hills which Lefty James had mentioned showed against the still-light sky, and the trail wove in and out, seeming at times to loop back on itself.

Their first warning was a shot. The bullet, fired from a high bank to the left, screamed out over their heads. Sandson, in the lead, halted his horse, holding the nervous animal motionless as he stared at the distant bluff.

"Who is it?"

"You know who it is!" Que Layton's voice rolled down to them like thunder. "I've got fifty guns covering you! Ride back!"

Several of the men had pushed up around Sandson, and Bruce Powell urged his horse forward. "It looks as if we've found them."

Sandson threw him an irritated glance and, swinging in his saddle, called to James. The hide hunter came up with marked reluctance, never taking his eyes from the bluff. "Can we rush them?"

James shrugged. "They'll murder you. The trail loops around that bluff and then cuts through the ridge. It's a three-quarter-mile ride and you'd be under their guns every foot of it."

Sandson swore. "Then what do we do?"

James' tone was without emotion. "There's three things you can do. You can ride back like that fellow says. You can camp. Or you can swing east and try to circle them."

"And after that?" Powell asked. "Wirt Downer's herd must be south of these hills. If we swing around Layton we'll be south too. All he will have to do is to hold the gap."

Impatience made Sandson's voice ragged. "You're a military man. What would you suggest?"

Powell held his temper. "Layton has us stymied, but supposing we leave most of the men on this side to wait for the chuck wagon. Two or three of us can circle through the hills and let Wert Downer know we're here. He probably has ten to fifteen hands. A few can hold the cattle, the rest can cut at the farmers from the south while you move against them from this side. They aren't going to like being cut off. They might run out of grub and water. I think that after two or three days sniping most of them might quit and head for home."

Sandson digested this in silence. He was not a man who liked waiting, but he could think of nothing better. "Who will make the circle?"

"I'll try," said Powell. "James had better come with me since he knows the country."

"And me," said Cappy.

Layton's voice reached them from the bluff, mocking them. "Well, is it run or fight?"

"Pull back a mile," Powell said. "Let them think we've gone. It will bother them all the more when they learn their error in the morning."

24.

NEVER AFTERWARD would Bruce Powell forget the ride through the badlands. The moon did not rise until they had covered most of the distance and the footing was so treacherous that they had to dismount and lead their horses most of the way.

It was well after midnight before they reached the pass which James had been hunting and crossed the ridge to start down the south flank of the hills. Cappy was stumbling with fatigue and had to be helped to his horse when they finally reached ground smooth enough for riding.

James halted, squinting upward at the distant stars. "The worst is over," he told Powell. "All we've got to do is follow this creek west toward Indian Wells."

His statement proved slightly optimistic, for they were forced to make long and tedious detours around cutbanks and gullies before they finally came out at the Wells. When they did they were in for a disappointment. There was no sign of Downer's herd.

"I give up," said Cappy, slipping to the ground and walking stiffly to the spring. "I'm through."

James had been studying the rutted earth. "Hasn't been any cattle along here." He shook his head. "Maybe they heard about those farmers and turned west somewhere south."

Cappy finished his long drink and straightened. "Probably they sold out to Daigle already and we had the ride for nothing."

Bruce Powell was stubborn. "They couldn't have driven them far yet. We'll ride south. At least we can find where they turned off if we don't find them." He swung his horse, not waiting for the groaning printer to remount.

They found the herd a good fifteen miles south. They sensed it long before they saw the bedded animals, hearing its restless movement, hearing the nighthawks as they circled slowly, singing to their uneasy charges. Then they spotted the fire and rode toward it, success making them forget their tired muscles.

"Hold up!" A guard had straightened from a wagon tongue, his rifle ready.

A man rose beyond the fire and moved out into the shadows, coming toward them. "Who are you?"

"Powell," the major said, "from Dexter Springs. I'm bringing you the men my brother promised." He stepped out of the saddle wearily and, without waiting to be asked, moved in toward the fire. Then he stopped, for he saw Clayton Daigle sitting beyond the small blaze. At Daigle's side, Tut Jackson squatted on his boot heels.

Bruce Powell's pause was only momentary; then he moved in with Cappy and James at his back. He heard Wirt Downer grumble an order for the cook to bring up cups and the blackened coffeepot, and felt the scalding liquid spread warmth down through his tired body as he drank.

Daigle had not moved. Tut Jackson had an open knife in his hand and was whittling on a twisted branch, giving his full attention to the operation.

Powell glanced around. Some of Wirt Downer's crew were asleep, although the light streak in the eastern sky showed that it was almost morning. They were as tense and nervous as a bunch of jumpy cats and their faces showed the dull tiredness which the endless miles of trail had brought. They were worn out from riding, and now, almost to their goal, they were blocked by the threat of the granger attack.

He knew exactly how they felt. He too had brought cattle up the long trail from Texas; he too had forded countless rivers, had fought storm and Indians and stampedes; and he had been almost finished when they finally drove their footsore charges into Dodge.

But there had been fight left in him, and there was still fight left in these men if he could arouse them. He looked around again, sensing the weight of their distrust. He knew that Daigle had without doubt told them of the embattled farmers camped on the ridge, had warned them that they would never get through with the herd. He felt Daigle's bright eyes on him, mocking him, even before he began to speak.

"I've got twenty gun fighters north of the sand hills," he said flatly. "Say the word and we'll clear the trail for you."

Wirt Downer was small, looking almost hunchbacked in the heavy brush jacket that was buttoned high against the night's cold. And he was as tired as his crew. There was weariness in his tone and the way he moved around the fire.

"Daigle tells us we haven't got a chance."

Powell did not even glance at Clayton Daigle. "Of course he'd tell you that. He wants to buy your herd, Downer. He planned this attack by the farmers in an effort to force you to sell at his price. He has his crew waiting, ready to take the cattle off your hands. That's no accident, you know."

"I know," said Downer, and the tone of voice was sharp as if he were asking if Powell took him for a fool.

Daigle stood up lazily. "I'm not trying to force anyone to do anything." His voice was smooth. "I am, frankly, taking advantage of a situation. That is only good business. The major does not like me for a number of reasons, but if he says that I am forcing you to sell, he's crazy. I'll buy, but the decision is yours. We're camped on Cottonwood Creek, west of here. When you make up your mind, send a rider to tell me." He turned then and moved to his horse.

Tut Jackson stood up. He leisurely put the knife back into its sheath, hitched his gun belt around into a more comfortable position and followed his employer. A minute later they spurred off into the darkness.

Wirt Downer listened to the fading sound of their horses, then looked back at the major. "You say your men are north of the ridge? Why aren't they here?"

"They can't get through."

"Then how can they help us with the cattle?"

"Look," said Bruce Powell. "I have twenty men north of the ridge. You have twelve or fifteen hands. Supposing we arranged to attack the farmers from both sides. How long do you think Layton's men would hold their position? They haven't much grub, and James tells me there's no water along the trail. A day, two days, and you'd see them heading for home, glad to go."

Downer chewed reflectively on a straw, his eyes on his tired crew. "Get some sleep," he said finally. "I want to think about it. We'll talk in the morning."

25.

QUE LAYTON was given to boasting. All his life he had dominated those around him. He was a bully, with all the instincts of a bully, all the desire for power which men of his type have. He was very pleased with himself as he sat on a rock beside the fire and watched the faces of the men around him.

"We've stopped them." His bull-like voice rose through the quiet night. "I promised you that not a Texas steer would cross these hills. They won't. Powell and Sandson have pulled back. They know better than to try to ride through the pass against fifty guns."

The farmers watched him, drawing from his strength in their uncertainty. Most of them were not fighting men. They had come west, seeking new homes, and they had ridden south only because they firmly believed that those homes were threatened by the coming of the Texas cattle.

A stone jug passed from hand to hand, each man having his heartening swig. Que Layton well understood the type of men he led. He was old, very experienced in border warfare. He knew that men such as these would fight fiercely for the few possessions that they owned, but he also knew that they were subject to letdown, to uncertainty, once a crisis was passed.

The liquor helped, robbing them of worry, easing the nerves which had been taut in expectation of the battle which had not yet developed.

He looked at his sons, dark and lean as Indians. They were good boys, he thought, who had learned their painful lessons well. But they were not leaders and never would be. It was, he reasoned, partly his fault. He had ordered their actions since the first day they could sit a horse. They had none of the restless drive which had carried him from one thing to another, none of the ambition which made it necessary to him that he have power.

And he meant to have power. He was not unconscious of Sandson's plans. He had watched the marshal closely ever since the man had come to Dexter Springs. At first he had thought that there might grow some alliance between them, but finally he realized that nothing would ever satisfy Deacon Sandson except complete domination.

On that day he had decided the man must go. Western Kansas was to belong to Que Layton and to no one else. He thought now of the marshal and his gun fighters camped along the trail. From the crest behind him he could see the winking light of their fire. But he felt that they constituted no threat. They were north of the hills, the cattle south. He expected that by morning he would have word that Clayton Daigle had purchased the herd and was turning it toward the state line.

He smiled as the jug was passed to him. He raised it to his bearded lips and drank deeply of the fiery liquor and felt the tongues of flame run down through his big body. Then he rose and made a slow circle of the camp.

Daigle had been very helpful. He had known Daigle when the man had his ranch in the Nations. There was complete and utter understanding between them. Had Daigle planned to remain in Kansas, they could not have been friends, since both were strong-willed, both absolutely self-centered. Sooner or later their interests would clash.

But Daigle was not remaining in Kansas. Daigle was pushing northward, planning to carve his own empire from the heartland of the Sioux. Let Daigle have his ranch, if he could hold it against the Indians. For Layton it was enough that he had emerged as a leader in the new granger movement. It would allow him to control this country, this section, perhaps even the state.

He took his saddle blanket and, retreating from the noise around the fire, rolled up in the shelter of a small dray. It was not too much to hope, he thought, that he might someday sit in the statehouse, put there by the farmer vote, administrating Kansas for the good of the farmers and of Que Layton. With that thought he went to sleep, his heavy lips parted by a little smile.

He did not hear the man who crept over the ridge behind him. He did not see the single flash of the knife as the intruder raised it and then plunged the heavy blade directly into the back just under the left shoulder.

He cried out once, trying to raise himself, and then fell back heavily. He was dead before his sons could reach him.

26.

UNCONSCIOUS OF Que Layton's death, Bruce Powell slept lightly for two hours until the slanting rays of the sun on his face wakened him. He lay for a moment trying to orient himself and then sat up.

The camp was almost deserted. The cook puttered around the chuck wagon and the gear was scattered about, showing plainly that they had no intention of moving that morning.

Powell kicked out of his blanket and rose stiffly, turning to look at the herd which had been spread out across the thin grass to feed. They ranged almost as far as eye could reach, and here and there he caught a flash of color as a rider moved slowly through the grazing stock.

The major turned and moved in to the wagon, finding Lefty James seated, his back to a high wheel, nursing a cup of hot coffee in his twisted hands.

"Where's Downer?"

The cook turned from the fire to indicate the scattered cattle with a sweep of his hand. "Out there. You wake the fat man and I'll give you breakfast."

Powell stooped and heaved a small stone at Cappy's head. He missed, striking the big shoulder. Cappy groaned, his eyes still closed. He turned, pulling the blanket tighter around his chin.

Powell threw a second pebble, striking the center of the bald head. Cappy came upright with a roar; then seeing the major grinning at him he sheepishly put on his hat and moved stiffly to the fire. "My old mammy told me this would happen if I left Ohio," he complained. "A man should have a bed. The ground is too hard."

Powell did not bother to answer. The cook was already filling the plates. He took one and emptied it rapidly. Then he turned out and, with Lefty's help, saddled the horses while Cappy finished. They rode out, passing the scattered trail crew. The riders were making no effort to drive the cattle, merely letting them drift a little northward.

Finally they found Downer away out on the western point, jogging slowly beside one of his men. He saw them coming and hauled up to wait for their approach. "Morning."

"Morning," said Powell and checked his horse. "Any news?"

"I sent a rider north to check on what you said. Those farmers are all over those hills. He watched them from the Wells before he came back."

"I told you that this morning."

Wirt Downer squinted at his scattered herd. "There's nigh onto three thousand critters," he was talking to himself, "and we brung them a long, weary way. I'd sure hate to be turned back now. I'd be plumb busted."

Cappy Ayers said in a disgusted voice, "What's this talk about turning back? I always heard Texans were fighters."

Wirt Downer squinted at him with an old man's wisdom. "I've fought some against the Mexicans," he mused, "and some against the Yankees, to say nothing about the brush jumpers that bothered us on the first drives into Missouri. And then there was a few Indians. I guess maybe I'm just a little tired."

Powell knew how the man felt. *I guess I've been a little tired myself ever since the war.* And Downer was getting old. This was perhaps his last drive. He would not come up the trail again.

Aloud he said, "There's only one way to clear those farmers from the hills. With your men moving in from the south and Sandson and his riders bring pressure from the north, a lot of them are going to want to quit. Three or four days of it and Layton won't have anyone left except his sons and a few die-hards, but you'll have to fight."

"Unless I sell to Daigle," Wirt Downer said.

Bruce Powell looked at him. "He won't pay more than half of what I can give you at the railroad."

Wirt Downer said slyly, "You could buy the herd here and drive it in yourself."

Powell grinned in spite of himself, deciding that Downer would make a good hand at a poker table. "I couldn't," he said. "I'm buying with bank credits and my contract states definitely that I can't purchase an animal until it's delivered to the loading pens. Why not put it up to your crew—offer them a bonus if you get through?"

The old man shook his head. "They're good kids, only two of them over twenty, and they'd drive into hell if I asked it.

103

But I won't ask it. I guess I'll settle with Daigle. There will be other herds up the trail, Major."

Powell knew from the flat tone that Downer had come to his decision the hard way, but now that it had been reached the old man would be slow to change his mind. "The other trail bosses will hear about you turning back," he said. "They'll hesitate to drive this far."

He did not add that if Downer sold to Daigle the game was lost, that Dexter Springs would never be a shipping point. He turned his horse, then stopped, for Lefty James was pointing toward the right.

"Company," the hide hunter said, "and coming fast."

Wirt Downer swung around, cursing under his breath. "The durn fools! Don't they know how to ride through cattle? We'll have a stampede on our hands." He started toward the approaching man, with the others following.

Powell recognized the marshal while a good eighth of a mile separated them. He wondered what Sandson was doing south of the hills, and then he realized that the two riders behind Sandson were Laytons, and his frown deepened. What were old Que's sons doing riding with the marshal?

Downer had pushed ahead, and he reached Sandson first, his faded blue eyes blazing. "What are you trying to do, run my herds? I ought to knock you out of that saddle."

Sandson paid no attention to the cattleman. He pushed on until he came abreast of Powell. Dropping his hand, he pulled the gun from his hip and laid its six-inch barrel across his saddle horn so that it pointed directly at the major's stomach.

"Cover Cappy and the others."

Both Laytons spoke at once, grimly, "We got them." Their guns were out, their hard eyes watching Cappy, Downer, James and the D 7 rider. "No moves."

Sandson ignored them, keeping his attention centered on Powell. "Pull your guns slow, Major. Let them drop."

Powell made no move to obey. He said in a controlled voice, "Maybe this makes sense to you, Sandson. It had better."

"It does," said Sandson. "I'm telling you once more to let those guns drop. Otherwise I'll shoot you out of the saddle."

Bruce Powell had faced death a number of times, but he knew that he had never come closer to dying than at that moment. He could read desire in the marshal's flaming eyes, the hatred there, the mounting wildness. He held his reins in his right hand, watching Sandson's eyes as he dropped his left hand on the worn stock of one heavy gun and lifted it slowly from its holster.

His whole impulse was to flip the heavy barrel, to take his chances with Sandson then; but he held himself, forcing his fingers to relax so that the gun fell to thump against the sandy ground at the horse's feet. Then he dropped the other and finally raised his left hand shoulder-high in a gesture which could not be mistaken.

"What is this, Deacon, a sellout?" he asked quietly.

Sandson's eyes were glowing. He glanced at Wirt Downer and decided that the old cattleman would not take any part. He sat by, quiet and natural, his gloved hands crossed on his saddlehorn. The D 7 man was motionless, watching, curious without real interest. Cappy had let his shotgun drop to the ground and was half slumped in the saddle, looking as if he might fall from sheer exhaustion. It was Lefty James who caught Sandson's attention, and the marshal said in a colorless tone.

"Who are you with, Lefty?"

James shifted his cud and spat thoughtfully. "I stay bought," he said without emotion. "You hired me, Deacon. You ought to know."

Sandson was obviously relieved. "Good. Get their guns." He indicated Downer and the D 7 rider with a jerk of his head.

James swung his horse around. He lifted Wirt Downer's gun, then repeated the performance with the rider.

Bruce Powell had not taken his eyes from Sandson. He said, still in his controlled voice. "I asked you a question, Deacon. What is this, a sellout?"

"Major," said Sandson. "I told you once that I do not work for you. I work for the town. I take my orders from Andrew Hyde."

"And he told you to do this, to ride with the Laytons? I don't think I understand."

"Don't you?" said Sandson. He reached into his saddle pocket and brought out a knife. He held it balanced in his hand for a moment, then he flipped it.

It fell, point first, burying its heavy blade in the soft earth almost to the hilt, the carved silver handle vibrating a little before it came to rest.

"Recognize it?" There was a hungry, eager note in Sandson's voice as if this were a moment he had waited for a long, long time.

Bruce Powell stared down at the standing knife. He had no difficulty in recognizing it. Anyone who had ever seen the beaten silver handle would know it at once. There was not another like it anywhere. It was his knife, the one the old Mexican had made for him before the war, the one he had carried for years, the one he had last seen lying on his desk in their offices above Len Milliard's store.

"Where'd that knife come from?"

The marshal's tone was like the lash of a whip. "Where you left it, Major. I pulled it out of Que Layton's back. His sons found his body this morning a hundred feet from his fire. They found him murdered with your knife. That's why I'm here, Major. I didn't sell out. I'm a law officer and I'm here to arrest you for that murder."

27.

FOR A moment no one moved, no sound came save the steady beat of the wind over the restless stomp of Downer's horse. Then Sandson bent down and, without leaving the saddle, pulled the knife from the ground and placed it in his pocket.

"Don't worry, Major. We aren't going to hang you here. I made a deal with the boys." He indicated the glowering, silent Laytons. "You're going back to the Springs for a trial, a fair trial, with a lot of farmers on your jury."

"So you did sell out." Bruce Powell sounded bitter. "You'll ride back to town leaving the grangers to hold the hills and Daigle to buy Downer's herd."

"Wrong." The marshal's thin lips twisted in a narrow smile. "These boys came out to meet me at daybreak, as soon as they found their father. They guessed someone from our camp was guilty. I recognized the knife, and I pointed out to them that I couldn't ride through to pick you up as long as they held the hills.

"I told you I made a deal. I went in with my men to talk to them, and got everything straightened out. The grangers have no leader, and without Que they've got no stomach for a fight. They're headed home now, glad to be out of it so easily. The hills are clear. Downer can drive his herd in and no one will stop them."

"There's one point," said Powell, "that you may have overlooked. I was with Cappy and James all night. We never separated. If I killed Layton, why, they did too. Are you going to try them along with me?"

"Not me," said James. The hide hunter had backed his horse out of the circle as if he had anticipated just such a need. The guns he had lifted from the rider and Downer were in his hands, covering both Sandson and the Laytons. "Drop them, quick."

Hugh Layton twisted convulsively, and the gun in James' right hand spoke, the heavy bullet catching Layton in the shoulder, knocking him clear of the saddle.

Cappy came bouncing from his horse like a rubber ball and grabbed the wounded man as he clawed desperately for his fallen gun.

"Behave." The fat man rolled him over and sat down on his chest, picking up the gun himself. "Can I shoot Sandson?"

The marshal was frozen in his saddle. Bruce Powell reached across and lifted the gun from Sandson's hand and the deacon made no effort to resist.

He said calmly, "My men and some of the grangers are at the D 7 camp. They'll hear the shot. You haven't any chance."

James had pushed forward and disarmed the other Layton. "We'll make out."

Sandson twisted to look at the hide hunter. "And I'll not forget this," he promised. "You lied. You said you stayed bought."

"Deacon," said James, "you aren't as smart as I thought in accusing Powell. You forgot that I was with him, that if he was guilty, I'd have to be guilty too."

"I didn't accuse you of anything."

"No," said the hunter, "but you would. Your story wouldn't hold up unless you did. What shall we do with them, Major?"

"Put them afoot," Bruce Powell said. "Get down, Sandson. Get down, all of you."

Sulkily the three climbed down.

"Better shoot the deacon," Cappy insisted. "You'll never have a finer chance."

Powell ignored him. The fat man scrabbled to his feet, went over and picked up his shotgun. Powell dismounted and gathered up the horses and swung back into the saddle. To Downer he said, "Sorry to put you afoot, but I haven't much choice. I'll see you in the Springs."

"No," said Sandson. "The minute you show up in the Springs you hang. After this you hang wherever we come up with you."

Powell didn't answer, but turned away, leading the horses. Lefty James followed, carrying the captured guns, and Cappy brought up the rear, muttering to himself. He had not been kidding. He believed that they should have shot the marshal when they had the chance.

An hour later they paused to draw breath. They had turned the captured horses loose with the guns tied to the saddles. Ahead of them rose the badlands, rougher here than they had been to the east, offering shelter, a place of concealment.

Lefty James squatted down beside the creek to have his drink, and straightened, wiping his mouth with the back of his hand. "If we had sense we'd drift right out of this part of the country. This chicken don't care for the signs. Some of them men with the deacon can trail with an Indian. There are twenty of them, to say nothing about those Layton boys and a few farmers. There's three of us."

Bruce Powell glanced at the sky. It was well past noon. He looked carefully back toward the east. There was no sign of dust, but with the ground as damp as it was there would be almost none.

"Those mining camps down in the new Mexico don't ask too many questions." It was still James, talking as if thinking aloud.

"Won't do," said Cappy, glancing sidewise at the silent Powell. "The major can't run. There's a woman involved."

Powell turned slowly to look at the fat man, then faced the hunter. "Cappy's right," he said shortly. "There's a number of reasons why I can't leave this part of the country, but this isn't your fight. You signed on to guard the herds and that's finished. If I were in your shoes I'd get out of Kansas as fast as a horse could carry me."

James grunted. "Hell with it. I'm fifty-five years old and I've ridden this country from one end to the other for twenty-five years, not asking permission from white man or Indian. I'm a little too old to start now, even if Deacon Sandson has gone loco and calls us murderers."

"The deacon ain't loco," said Cappy. "I warned the major to watch out. I warned him that the next time Sandson came for him it wouldn't be direct. It would be kind of underhanded, like killing a man with a knife and then hanging the killing on the knife's owner."

"So that's what you think happened?" Powell turned to study the distance behind them.

Cappy spat. "What else would happen? That knife didn't just walk out into the hills by itself. You ain't carried it since you came to the Springs. It's been lying up on your desk, a-holding down papers."

"That's right."

"The marshal," said Cappy, "is a thoughtful critter. He figures and schemes and he tries to think ahead. He wants to be a big man in Dexter Springs, and he wants a girl. He can't have either as long as you're in his way, and he don't dare shoot you because Jenny would never speak to him again."

"We're wasting time," Powell cut in sharply, "and as usual you're talking too much."

Cappy paid no attention. "It all works out in Sandson's favor. He's practically killed four birds with one rock. You're finished. How long would it take a farmers' jury to have you strung up? And he's gotten rid of Que Layton. Without Layton, the farmers will wait for the legislature. They're going home and the cattle will drive into the Springs. The merchants will be happy to have the cowboy business without having made enemies of the farmers, and you'll wind up hanging by the neck, convicted of murder and blamed with everything that happened, and Sandson will have a clear shot at the girl with none to bother him."

"You've forgotten one thing," Bruce Powell told him. "You've forgotten Clayton Daigle. You've forgotten she is Daigle's wife."

"No," said Cappy. "I haven't forgotten she is Daigle's wife, but you've forgotten that Sandson doesn't know it. Sandson only knows that she wants the boy, and he will try to get the boy for her. It will be his ace. It is the only way he might have a chance with her. If you were Sandson, in Sandson's spot, what would you do? Wouldn't you raid Daigle's camp, kill Daigle if you could and take the boy back to Jenny?"

Powell said slowly, "I might, if I were Sandson."

"Of course you would," said Cappy. "There is nothing else that you could do. Everything is falling into place for

Sandson. He has the town. He has the power. He has you on the run. But he does not yet have the girl. The point is, are we going to sit by quietly and let him get her?"

Powell shook his head. "That's one thing I'm not going to let him get away with."

"And just how can you stop him?"

Powell's mouth twisted with bitterness. "I'm going to do something I hate to do. I'm going to join forces with Daigle. Under ordinary circumstances I should kill him because of Henry, but men aren't always free to do what they choose." He swung his horse around and headed for Cottonwood Creek. After a moment's hesitation the others followed.

28.

IT WAS nearly dark before they picked up the point of light which marked the fire beside Daigle's chuck wagon. The camp itself was fairly extensive, since Daigle had been prepared for the long drive north and was carrying supplies and a large remuda. It was sheltered in a small draw where a creek tumbled out of the badlands to join the larger stream.

Powell halted his horse a good mile away and, turning, watched his two companions as they drew up to his side. "If you're smart you'll ride around and head west. You can't help, and if I miss my play with Daigle we'll all be in bad trouble."

Lefty James eased himself in the saddle, staring down at the distant camp. "I suppose you know what you're doing, but I don't like it. No hard feelings if I ride on?"

"None," said the major, and brought his horse around and offered his hand. "I'll not forget what you did this morning."

James spat. "I never was much at doing favors and I wasn't then. In this country a man keeps his hair by tending his own business."

"Take Cappy with you," said the major. "He'll do no good here and he's too heavy to hang. It would take an extra rope."

The fat man started to protest, looked at Bruce Powell's eyes and changed his mind. He raised one pudgy hand and

Powell saw an ink stain running across its palm. Somewhere else, in some other town, Cappy would find a newspaper, but he doubted if the fat man would be as content as he had been on the *Enterprise*.

He sat his horse, watching the oddly matched pair turn down the hill and ride south so that they could circle Daigle's camp, and waited until they were well out of sight. Then he touched his tired horse with the spurs and dropped down toward the light of the campfire.

He made no effort at concealment, but swung into the tracked draw and up it toward the temporary rope holding corral, noting the long line of picketed animals.

Tut Jackson saw him first. The big foreman had been examining a horse and swung around, hearing Powell's approach. "Who is it?"

"Bruce Powell." His voice carried beyond the wagons and he saw Daigle appear at a half-run, coming toward him as the men who had been clustered around the fire turned.

He stepped from his saddle, walked his horse to the picket line and handed the reins to one of the guards. Then he turned and moved forward to meet the approaching Daigle.

He thought as he watched the group from behind the cattleman: *I never expected to walk into this camp. Some of these men shot Henry, some of them helped hold up that train and take Bobby from Jenny Paraine. This is the last place I would expect to be, the last place I would come for help.*

Daigle had recovered from his astonishment. His usual smile was in place, but his eyes in the firelight were glittering and watchful. It was obvious that he was suspicious of a trick.

"Well, Major." His voice held all the false heartiness which had made Powell dislike him from the first. "This is an unexpected pleasure, believe me. Step in. You're in time for food. Cook, another plate." He stood aside so Powell could come up to the fire.

Bruce Powell walked to the blaze, extending his hands and warming them.

"I'd hardly call it a pleasure," he said flatly. "I'd much prefer coming in behind a gun. There's a lot between us, Daigle, a lot that isn't settled."

Daigle made a tiny bow. "I judge that you did not ride through the hills merely to tell me that."

"I did not," said Bruce Powell. "I came to bring you a

warning. But before you get any suspicions about my motive, let me say that I had no choice. They are hunting me like a dog and if they find me I'll hang at the end of a rope."

He saw the flicker of surprise in Daigle's eyes. He had chosen his position purposely, his back to the fire so the jumping light fell directly on Daigle's face.

"And who is getting ready to hang you?" the man said.

"Sandson, and the crew of hardcases we brought in to guard the herd."

Daigle started to laugh. For once there was nothing forced in the man's merriment. He laughed until tears sprang into his eyes, and he was joined by Jackson and the circling crew.

"Your pardon," said Daigle when he could manage words. "But you'll have to admit, Major, that there is some irony in the situation—your own guards turning against you and you having to ride into my camp for help."

"To offer help," Powell corrected him. "Fighting makes strange bedfellows, as I learned in the late war, and unless I miss my guess you are going to need help before the night is out."

He watched the laughter die out of Daigle's eyes, leaving them clear and hard and alert. "What kind of a game is this?"

"No game," he said, and glanced around at the gathered men. "Sandson's next move will be to ride down on you, to wipe you out."

"Wipe us out? But . . ."

"There are several things I'd say if we were alone," Powell told him. "If you will take a short walk with me . . ."

"Don't do it," Tut Jackson said sharply. "You can't trust him, Clate. He might want to even things for his brother. This may be his way."

For answer the major reached down, unbuckled his gun belts and handed them to the big foreman. "All right?"

"All right," said Daigle, and led the way out beyond the picket line. "But the story had better be good."

"It's good enough," Powell said shortly. "It puts you out of this business, Daigle. Your fine scheme has fallen to pieces. Que Layton is dead, and the farmers are picking up and heading home. By tomorrow night Wirt Downer's herd will be through the badlands on its way to Dexter Springs."

Daigle stopped and turned. Here the light was not sharp enough for Powell to see the man's eyes, but he sensed the vibrating anger in the voice. "If this is a joke . . ."

112

"It isn't any joke," the major said. "Que Layton was murdered last night—with my knife. Sandson says I did it. The Layton boys are after my scalp."

"Did you kill him?"

"I did not. I don't expect you to believe me. I don't care what you believe, and I pretend no grief because of his death. He got exactly what he deserved. He has been a murdering raider along the Kansas border for twenty years, but his death is the end of your plans. His sons have made a deal with Sandson. All they want is to be avenged. They don't care whether Texas cattle drive into the railroad or not. They merely want to hang me."

"And you expect me to protect you?"

"I can protect myself," the major said calmly. "But the rest concerns you as much or more than it does me. Sandson is driven by two ambitions. One is to control western Kansas. At the moment it looks as if he is in control. The second one is not so easy. He wants to marry your wife."

For an instant Daigle was silent; then he broke into a soft laugh.

"It's not funny," Bruce Powell told him. "Sandson has plenty of power. He's a hero. He has opened the way to bring the cattle into the Springs without a fight. The merchants will love him for that, and if he succeeds in hanging me the farmers will love him for it. But none of these things will impress Jenny. There is only one thing she wants—her boy."

Daigle said with a hint of contempt. "Jenny will never look at Sandson."

"Probably not," Bruce Powell admitted, "but Sandson cannot believe that. He doesn't know she is your wife. He only knows that she wants the boy. He will try to take him from you."

Daigle looked at him curiously. "And just where do you come into this? You have had trouble with Sandson, but you have also had trouble with me. You did not bring this warning out of any kindness. What are you trying to gain? Are you merely saving your own skin?"

A slow smile curved Powell's lips and in the faint light from the distant fire his face was cold and ruthless. "I'm hoping you and Sandson will kill each other. If you do, it will save me the trouble of doing the job myself."

Daigle's laughter shattered the quiet of the night, echoing back to his watching crew, making them stir uneasily. "Major," he said when he could speak, "I've watched you in these

113

last three months as I've watched all the men in Dexter Springs. I tried to size you up, and I found it hard to fit you into the reputation you had gained during the war. I thought you were soft and vacillating. I begin to believe I was wrong."

"Situations change people," Powell said shortly. "I've watched many men change in the stress of battle, in the galling bitterness of defeat. I could have shot you from any of these surrounding hills. I could have killed Sandson this morning, but it would only have marked me with another murder and kept me from everything I hope for. It is much better to pit you two against each other."

"And then kill the survivor?" The mockery was back in Daigle's tone. "I almost like you, Major. I almost wish we had been together. Together we could have taken anything from this country that we wanted."

Bruce Powell almost said, *You don't understand. You don't want the same things I want. You're interested in buying cattle for a song, in stocking a new range as cheaply as you can, in gaining wealth and power. All I want is a chance to build a quiet life, a little peace, a chance to make up for the years that I lost fighting.*

But he did not speak. There was a gulf between him and Daigle which would never be bridged, a lack of common ground which yawned like a canyon between them.

"We'll see what happens," he said and started to turn away.

Daigle put a hand on his arm. "Wait. If you didn't kill Layton, who did? Was it Sandson? It seems to have fitted neatly into his plans."

"I couldn't prove it," said Bruce Powell and went back to the fire. Daigle followed him, the waiting riders parting to let them pass.

"These two men who were with you last night. They'd be witnesses in your favor. Where are they?"

"Gone," said Powell. "Whatever good they might do me as witnesses is counterbalanced by the danger that, if I hung for Layton's death, they would probably hang too." He turned and looked around the camp.

"Is your boy here?"

"Asleep in that wagon." Daigle pointed to a canvas-covered wagon beyond the fire. "When do you think Sandson will strike?"

Bruce Powell shrugged. "I have no way of knowing," he

114

said, "but if my guess is right he'll hit you tonight. You have no objection if I take back my guns?"

Daigle shook his head. "If you're telling the truth we can probably use a couple extra. If you aren't, it won't matter. There are fourteen men in this camp and I think we can handle you among us."

Powell did not answer. He walked across to where Tut Jackson had laid his gun belts on the wagon tongue and cinched them around his flat hips. Then he walked over to the wagon, pulled the canvas cover aside, and peered in.

Bobby Daigle lay curled up in a small knot, his body hardly making a bulge in the covering blankets. He slept, undisturbed by the sounds of the camp, one small fist tightly balled against his mouth.

Powell let the cover fall back into place and turned to find that Daigle was watching him sardonically. "You wouldn't have the same idea as Sandson perhaps—of grabbing the boy and taking him back to Jenny?"

"I'd thought of it," Powell said, "but I'm not exactly free to ride into the Springs, remember?"

"Why, that's right," said Clayton Daigle. "That gives me a small idea of my own. After we dispose of Sandson, it might be wise to hang you, after all."

29.

THEY HAD no more warning than if it had been an Indian attack. One minute the night was quiet; the next it was filled with hideous, explosive sound.

Powell had been asleep under one of the wagons. For the first part of the night they had kept a careful watch, but as the hours dragged on and there was no sign of Sandson's men, both Daigle and Tut Jackson watched him with growing suspicion, and the crew who had been standing guard relaxed.

But the attack had come. Sandson's men had crept up on the two guards who had turned careless and shot both of them before they knew anyone was about.

Tut Jackson was on his feet, kicking the embers of the fire

apart as he fired off into the darkness. As Powell emerged, Jackson turned and at that instant a bullet crashed into his stomach, dropping him like a folding jackknife into the hot ashes at his feet. Powell rushed across the trampled ground and seized the foreman's shoulders, dragging him from the coals. But he might have saved himself the trouble. Jackson was dead.

Other men died before they could free themselves from their blankets, and a bullet tore away Powell's hat as he dived under the wagon and came up on the far side, striking his head on Daigle's knees.

Clayton Daigle had pulled his son from the wagon box and was wrapping him in a blanket. He swore hoarsely as a bullet tore through the canvas cover and headed around the wagon.

Powell caught his shoulder. "The creek bed. Quick!"

Daigle turned and ran, hunched over so that his body offered some protection to the whimpering boy.

Behind them all was confusion, sharp cries of the crew as they tried to reach the horses, the stamping, circling, neighing animals, the hammer of shots from the still unseen attackers.

Ahead of Daigle a man rose up suddenly out of the darkness, a shadow, shapeless and indistinct. He fired point-blank at the cattleman. Daigle hesitated and missed a step, then went on.

Bruce Powell shot over Daigle. He heard the man yell and saw him fade out of their path. He almost stepped on the soft body as he ran by.

Daigle had reached the creek and dropped down over the edge of the cutbank. Powell went after him, sliding down the damp mud until his feet lit in the running water. The creek was not more than a foot deep, but it had cut a trough out of the sandy loam which was a good six feet below the surface of the surrounding draw.

"Upstream," Powell panted. "Let's try for higher ground."

Daigle did not answer. He was down on hands and knees, trying to crawl through the water, trying to carry the boy in the crook of his arm.

Powell reached over and took the blanketed child from him, and Daigle made no protest. "I'm hit." His voice was little more than a croak. "I'm hit bad. I guess you win the game. You win if you get out of here alive."

He slumped forward into the water, face down.

Powell pulled him out onto the bank and rolled him over. Daigle said weakly, "Go on. Take the boy and go on."

Noise above Powell jerked him erect and he spun to see a horseman outlined against the lighter sky. The man fired, the bullet kicking up a spit of water on Powell's right. He snapped a shot in return, saw the man fall sidewise, and scrambled up the slippery bank in an effort to catch the horse. It shied away and two men charged out of the darkness from the direction of the camp. He knocked the first out of the saddle and the other pulled to the right, the riderless horse following.

Powell hesitated for a moment. The whole night was a medley of running sound. Men shouted at one another, horses pounded across the rough ground, guns flamed in the darkness. It was impossible to tell friend from foe, even to guess how the fight was going.

He dropped back down into the creek, standing at the edge of the cold, running water. The mud of the bottom sucked greedily at his boots as he bent over Daigle.

The cattleman had managed to sit up. He said weakly, "The boy . . ."

Powell picked up the small blanket-wrapped figure, heard the child whimper and whispered to it soothingly. Daigle was struggling to get to his feet, and Powell said in an undertone, "Can you walk?"

"I can try." There was a deep stubbornness in the words. Daigle stepped out into the creek, moving carefully upstream. After a moment Powell followed, carrying the boy.

Their progress was painfully slow. The footing was treacherous, the sucking mud so deep that in spots they went in well above their boot tops. It seemed to Powell's straining ears that their noise should bring down all of Sandson's riders upon them, but the sound from the camp was like a heavy blanket, deadening all else.

The pitch of the creek's fall was sharp and the miniature canyon up which they toiled shallowed as they climbed to higher ground. Powell could see over the sheltering cutbanks without straightening.

The sky was blanketed with light clouds through which the moon broke at irregular intervals, and its light gave him an uncertain view of the rough hills which surrounded them.

Daigle coughed suddenly and went to his knees. He stayed

there a minute, unable to get up until Powell came to his aid. Put on his feet again, he managed to move ahead with the support of Powell's guiding arm.

They had covered perhaps another half-mile when Daigle went down again. This time Powell placed the boy on the shelving bank and used both arms to lift the cattleman from the creek.

"Can you go on?"

Daigle spoke with labored difficulty. "In a minute. If I can rest a minute . . ."

They rested, much longer than a minute. From where they sat they could stare down the narrow draw to where the camp had been. As they looked, flames leaped up into the night. Daigle swore in weakness and anger.

"They're burning the wagons."

Powell did not answer. His eyes were on the distant camp, trying to make out the figures which moved like flitting shadows around the leaping fire. He failed. It was impossible to recognize any of them, but the odds were good that they were Sandson's men. Daigle's crew would certainly never burn their own wagons.

"It looks like your boys took a thorough licking," he said, "in which case we aren't far enough away. It will be daylight in less than two hours, and we've got to find a place to hole up before then. If I know Sandson, he'll search this ridge thoroughly."

Without a word Daigle struggled to his feet and moved on up the hill, turning away from the creek now and mounting the rising ground, sometimes standing erect, but as often down, climbing on his hands and knees.

The basic stubbornness of the man was amazing. Powell thought that if he had to, Daigle would inch forward on his belly.

Powell followed, carrying the boy, conserving his strength for the time when Daigle's would give out completely. The going grew steadily worse, and they lost direction, pushing forward as the moon vanished behind another cloud bank, guided only by the ever rising contour of the hill.

They crossed the crest just before dawn. Their clothes, wet from the creek, had long since been grimed over with mud until they looked almost like part of the irregular landscape. In the increasing light Powell looked at Daigle and realized that the man was through, that he could not go much farther.

He found a little depression between some rocks and, taking the blanket from the boy, rigged it as a shelter. He scraped up the sandy soil in handfuls, tossing it across the blanket until the dull gray of the cloth was masked and blended into the hillside. Then he crawled under one edge of the shelter.

Daigle sat, his back against a rock, refusing to lie down, his heavy, handsome face drawn and white-looking, his eyes deep-sunk. For the first time Powell had a chance to look at the hole in the man's side and guess how much blood Daigle had lost during the night.

The man, he concluded, had the constitution of an ox, or he would have been dead long before. He used Daigle's own shirt to rig a kind of bandage over the blue-rimmed hole. He knew that it would do little good, but Daigle seemed cheerful and alert.

"I'm all right," he said. "It will take more than this to kill Clayton Daigle. That's something that Sandson is going to find out. As soon as I can stay on my feet I've got a small date to keep with that marshal."

30.

THE FIRST of the returning farmers brought Que Layton's body back to Dexter Springs. Pete Layton, his broken arm still in a sling, rode beside the horse which carried his father, looking young and grim and angry.

It was the first word that had reached the town about the happenings in the Sand Hills to the south, and a crowd gathered outside Montgomery's undertaking parlor.

The youngest Montgomery boy was sent to the hotel with a message for Edna Layton, and the girl rose to dress hurriedly.

Jenny Paraine had been sitting beside Henry Powell's bed, relieving Horndyke. She heard the commotion in the hall and opened the door just as Edna appeared from her room.

"What's happened?"

The younger girl's face was set. "It's my father," she said in a low voice. "He's dead. Pete sent word for me to come down to Montgomery's."

"Wait," said Jenny. She called one of the other girls to sit with Henry and went after her shawl.

Together they left the hotel and, crossing to Kansas Avenue, walked rapidly down the slatted sidewalk and turned into the long, bare room.

Pete was there, standing with some of his friends. He pushed through the crowd and put his good arm around his sister. He was nearer her age then either of the other brothers and in this moment the shock of grief drew them closer together than they had ever been.

"What's happened, Pete?"

"He was murdered," Pete Layton said. "He was knifed as he slept, with never a chance to fight back."

Jenny Paraine was standing just beyond Edna, but Pete paid no attention. "It was that damn cattle buyer, Powell. He crept up into the hills and murdered him."

"No." The word was torn from Jenny Paraine without her even realizing that she had spoken.

Pete looked at her then, his dark eyes narrowed and black with hurt and hate. "Yes. His knife was still in Que's back. He didn't even bother to pull it out and carry it away."

"I don't believe you," Jenny Paraine said heatedly. "There must be some mistake."

"There's no mistake." Pete Layton's bitterness grated into his voice. "Ever since those damn Southerners came into this country they've caused nothing but trouble—them with their stockyards and loading pens, riding down the trail to talk the herd drivers into coming into this country. They were willing to do anything to bring in those cattle, and they knew that they'd never succeed as long as Que lived. The simple way was to murder him."

His sister had pushed out of the circle of his arm. "I don't believe you either." Her voice was not as vehement as Jenny's, but she was just as positive. "I know there's been some mistake."

"There's no mistake." Pete Layton was thoroughly angry now. "What's the matter with you, Eddie? Your own father lies in there murdered and you speak up for his murderer. I think you've gone crazy."

"But how can you know?" Edna was facing him. "Did someone see Bruce Powell do the killing? Couldn't someone else have stolen the knife and used it? You're the one who's crazy."

"I'm not the only one then." Pete Layton turned to look

at the crowded room. Everyone there was silent, listening. "Even the marshal admitted Powell was the man, and you certainly don't think Sandson is a friend of ours, do you?"

Jenny Paraine started to say, *And you certainly do not think that Deacon Sandson is a friend of Powell's, do you?* But she checked herself. She realized that it was pointless to attempt to argue with this boy.

Instead she said, "Where is the deacon now?"

"He rode south after Powell," Pete Layton said. "My brothers went with him, and they'll bring that cattle buyer in. He hasn't got a chance."

John Kleban had been standing behind the girls. He asked now in a quiet voice, "What happened to Sandson's men? How come you boys aren't still in the hills?"

Layton turned sullen under the questioning. "Without my father, the farmers wouldn't stay and fight. Even my brothers didn't care. I tried to get them to stay, but they wouldn't listen. They traded with Sandson. They agreed not to block the herds if he would bring Powell in."

Jenny Paraine turned away, but before she reached the door Edna Layton pressed to her side. The room behind them was filled with talking men, excited by the news Layton had brought. She stepped outside and waited until Edna joined her, and they stood thus for a long moment looking at each other in the darkness.

A voice from the building corner said, "Your pardon, ladies, but would you tell me what happened inside?"

They turned to see Frenchy Armaud step into the light thrown from the half-open doorway. He stood now, a quiet, respectful man, his broad hat crumpled in his hand.

Jenny Paraine told him. She told him of the charge against Bruce Powell, of Que Layton's death, of the farmers pulling out of the hills.

The saloonkeeper listened with careful attention. "And Sandson? Where is the marshal?"

"He's gone south to arrest Bruce." Her voice caught a little over the name. "Hasn't Bruce had enough to stand without this, his brother shot and all the trouble . . ."

"And the brother?" said Frenchy. "Horndyke tells me he will live, that he will get well."

"I . . . I don't know. He's very weak, but the doctor seems confident."

"The doctor is a good man," said Frenchy Armaud, "and as for the major, do not start worrying about him until you

121

have to. Bruce Powell is also a good man. He has been through a great deal and survived. My money will be on him and not on Sandson. The marshal is a dangerous man, but he has his weaknesses. We all have our weaknesses. Sometimes they trip us up." He replaced his hat then and moved away from them toward the railroad.

Jenny Paraine stared after him. Something in his quiet manner brought reassurance, a reassurance she needed badly at the moment. Edna was clinging to her arm. The younger girl was not crying, but the shock of the evening had been heavy. They moved back toward the hotel.

31.

TWICE DURING the day Bruce Powell made the trip from their improvised shelter to the creek, bringing back water in his hat. The hours dragged by. He spent most of them lying on his stomach watching the surrounding country. During the morning he saw half a dozen horsemen apparently riding aimlessly through the rough country, but never were they close enough to be recognized.

In the afternoon he saw no one and, as dusk approached, he said to Daigle, "Looks like friend Sandson has given up. He probably figures you got a horse and cleared out of the country."

Daigle's eyes were fever-bright, and there was a flush over his high cheekbones. He'd half lain, half sat, all during the day under the shelter of the blanket.

The boy had been restless, then hungry. Powell had tried to distract him, taking him outside to crouch at his side as he scanned the country.

Now the boy slept, exhausted after the long night and the napless day, and Bruce Powell looked at the small face. There was a lot of Jenny Paraine in that face, the way the eyes were shaped and the way the long lashes curled back. Bobby certainly looked a great deal more like his mother than his father.

"We can't stay here forever," Powell said. "You need a

doctor and we need food. As soon as it's dark I'll cut back down to the camp and see what I can find—or better still, start out and see if I can reach Downer's outfit. They may be through the hills, but they can't have moved too far north yet. I'll take the boy and . . ."

He stopped, for Clayton Daigle had shifted his position slightly, uncovering the gun which had been concealed beneath his arm. "You don't take the boy." He raised the gun so that it covered Bruce Powell fully. "Bobby stays here with me."

Powell stared at him. "Have you lost your mind?"

"Not yet," said Daigle. Despite his pain he managed a tiny smile. "It would be very nice if you went out of here carrying the boy, very convenient for you if I lay here and died . . ."

"You fool!" Powell's patience was worn thin. "I'm coming back. I have no intention of leaving you here for good."

"I know you're coming back," Daigle said, "because the boy stays here with me and you could never in this world face Jenny if you left him out in these hills to die."

Powell hesitated, half tempted to jump the wounded man, to wrest the gun from his grasp. Daigle read the thoughts in his eyes.

"Don't try it," he said weakly. "I'm still not so far gone that I can't shoot."

"All right," said Powell, and turned out of the makeshift shelter. Behind him Daigle crawled to the entrance and squatted there holding the gun. Powell looked back once and then started down the hill.

There was still enough light for him to see the rough footing and he made quick progress to the creek, turning down it as the easiest way to descend the draw.

He came opposite the campsite about full dark, climbed the bank warily and walked through the litter of the place. He had half hoped that he would find some food, overlooked by the raiders, or perhaps a horse grazing in the small bottom land; but the only animals he located were dead, and Sandson's men had ruthlessly piled all the supplies upon the fire so that nothing remained save the charred and blackened ashes.

He stood for a moment, cursing the marshal for his thoroughness. Sandson had known that the best way to drive Daigle's remaining hands from the country was to wipe out their supplies. He thought of Daigle up on the ridge, of the sleeping, hungry boy, and his jaw set as he started southward along the foot of the rise.

He was not used to walking. The ground was rough, and he had eaten nothing since the preceding evening. But he held on grimly, mile after mile, at times plunging down into sharp gullies which ran toward the flatland, at others circling far out of his way to cross a particularly steep bank.

His progress was slow. He covered little better than a mile an hour, and the eastern sky already showed light and rosy when he reached the trail at Indian Wells.

He paused at the spring to drink, and then moved on to where the marks of thousands of hoofs had chewed up the still damp ground.

Wirt Downer's herd had passed and moved on through the hills. A few days ago that knowledge would have brought its high feeling of relief, but now he was almost too tired, too worn out to care.

He turned, following the trail as it climbed gradually through the pass, reaching the crest and starting down the north slope. He passed the point at which Que Layton had halted them, then came out of the broken land and saw the grazing animals spreading before him.

One of the drag riders spotted him and came spurring across, made tense and nerve-edged by the events of the last two days.

"Well, look who's here," he said. "There's been men hunting the country for you, and you walk into my hands." His gun was out and he covered Powell carefully. "No tricks."

Bruce Powell was too tired to care. He sat down beside the trail, looking up at the mounted rider. "Tell Downer there's a wounded man and a kid ten miles back. They have no food and they're going to die if someone doesn't get to them."

The rider stared down at him. He hesitated, trying to make up his mind, and then it seemed to occur to him that Powell was afoot and not likely to go far. He swung his mount and went racing away toward the distant wagons which were already out of sight.

Powell watched him go without too much interest. He was so bone-weary that nothing held much importance. He lay back, relaxing, afraid to pull out of his boots, knowing that he would never get them on again. He roused from a half-stupor into which he'd drifted and realized that four men were riding toward him and came slowly to his feet. He had

124

no real idea of how long it had been since the man had gone for Downer. It could not have been too long, although the sun was well up in the morning sky.

Instinctively his hand dropped to one of his holstered guns. Before, he had been played out, too tired to even try to fight back. But the rest, short as it had been, had tapped the reservoir of his reserve strength and he was clear-headed and alert again.

But there was no need for guns. The men with Downer were the cattleman's own riders, and the little trail boss showed no hostility. He looked at the major, bearded and mud-caked, and swung down.

"Looks like it's been a little rough."

"A little," said the major, and told Downer what had happened.

The trail boss had brought a pail of hot coffee and two saddlebags of food, and Powell ate while he talked. When he finished the trail boss shook his head.

"I didn't like Sandson's looks," he said. "Some of his crew passed us this morning, headed north. I gathered that the rest had cut through the hills, hunting you. Where is this boy and Daigle?"

"No one would ever find them," Powell said. "I'll have to ride back myself, but if you could let me have a man and a couple of horses I'd appreciate it."

A half-hour later he was headed again through the hills, a D 7 rider behind him leading an extra horse. They made good time and the sun was not entirely gone when they passed the burned-out camp and climbed along the stream toward the blanket shelter. The shelter was still there and Powell swung down, calling Daigle's name. He got no answer and quickly crossed to pull the blanket away.

Daigle was there, lying where he had sat during the night, unmoving and unseeing, his body already cold. There was no sign of the boy.

Bruce Powell swung around, calling Bobby's name. He got no answer and moved in a circle, looking at the ground. The tracks of two horses came in from the left and stopped beyond the rocks behind the shelter.

Boot heels had made marks in the soft ground where the riders had dismounted; then the tracks of the men returned to the horses and stopped. Whoever they were, they had re-mounted and headed northward through the hills, taking Bobby with them.

125

32.

IT WAS long after midnight before they got back to Wirt Downer's camp. Bruce Powell stepped from the saddle, the sap drained out of him. He drank almost a quart of the cook's scalding coffee and ate slowly, squatted down against the wagon wheel while the crew circled about him, listening as he and Downer talked.

"Must have been Sandson's men," Downer said. "Two riders, huh, and headed north?"

Powell nodded. Weariness flowed over him, making the top section of his head a little light as if it lacked the blood to make his brain function properly.

"At least the boy is safe."

He thought about that slowly and decided that Downer was right. Bobby was probably safe, even now in Jenny's arms. He pictured Sandson riding in triumphant with Bobby before him on the saddle.

Sandson had won. The whole game was in his hands. But Bruce Powell knew with a gritty forcefulness that he would never rest until Sandson was stopped.

The man was like a mad dog, drunk with power. The utter ruthlessness with which he had attacked the Daigle crew, willing to slaughter a dozen men if it furthered his purpose, was the tip-off to the marshal's state of mind. Whatever else happened, Bruce Powell meant to keep him away from Jenny Paraine. The girl had suffered enough without being exposed to the marshal's callousness.

He slept finally, curled up in a borrowed blanket, knowing that for what he had to do he needed strength, a certain hand and a clear mind.

In the chill gray of the early morning he breakfasted with Downer's men, and, having finished, asked for the loan of a horse.

As always, at the start of the day, Wirt Downer was grumpy, irascible and taciturn. He looked at Powell now, shaking his head. "How far is it into the Springs?"

"From here I'd guess between thirty and forty miles."

126

"You'd better wait," said Downer, "until we get the herd closer, until I can send some men in with you. That Sandson has all the cards in the deck. Alone you wouldn't have a chance."

Powell turned to look at him fully. "I don't understand." He said it slowly. "Two nights ago I wanted you to use your crew to fight the farmers and you refused. Now you're offering me help."

"Damn it," said Downer and spat angrily, "I wouldn't send the boys to die merely to bring the cattle through, merely to save me money. This is different. You're a Texan and you're in deep trouble, and when has any Texan sat idly by and let one of his own ride without help?"

Bruce Powell's drawn face cracked into a smile and he put out a big hand which Downer took slowly. "I'll not forget that," he said. "But right now I need a horse, not a crew. There aren't enough Texans this side of the Red to take that town by force. One man has a chance to ride in. A dozen would be stopped before they crossed the river."

Downer squinted at him, then swore under his breath. "Be it on your own head," he said. "Charlie, catch the major up a horse. Better make it two. He'll probably kill the first one before he's gone fifteen miles."

33.

DEACON SANDSON came into Dexter Springs a good twenty-four hours after Pete Layton had arrived with Que Layton's body. He found the town quiet and, after quartering the eleven riders he still had with him, he sought out Andrew Hyde. Together they walked to the mayor's office.

"It's this way," said Sandson when they were seated. "The farmers are dispersed. Without leadership they aren't apt to give us further trouble."

"And Powell? What about this murder?"

"What about it?" said Sandson, and his eyes glowed a little.

The mayor told him hastily, "I'm not questioning you. I merely asked. Will it stick?"

"The farmers believe it," said Sandson, "and Powell has few friends. How is the brother?"

"Horndyke thinks he'll live, but it will be a long time before he is out of bed. We need not worry about him. It was a lucky thing for us that old Layton died."

"A very lucky thing," Sandson agreed, and gave him a thin-lipped smile. "Luck follows those who make it, Andrew, and we make our own. I think now it is time we went to call on Len Milliard. With the Powells out of the picture, there must be someone to buy the cattle, someone to ship them east, and the time is short. Downer should be in sometime next week." He rose, and the mayor followed him to the street and up the dark sidewalk toward the residential section.

Len Milliard had been asleep. He blinked at his late visitors, huddling his big form in a shabby robe. Sandson always worried him. The marshal was so quiet, yet so potentially dangerous.

"I'm glad to see you," he said, "and glad that the herds are coming through without a battle."

Sandson studied the merchant. He had nothing but contempt for Len Milliard and the man's penny-pinching ways, but he recognized Milliard's position and the man's power, and he wanted everything understood. His plans called for using Milliard as he had successfully used Hyde.

"The reason there was no fighting," he said, "was Que Layton's death. Had he lived I doubt whether any herd would ever have come through the hills."

"I never thought Bruce Powell would stoop to murder."

"Nor I," said Sandson, and grinned faintly. "But it is always possible to find a man to wield a knife if you have the money and know where to look."

Comprehension grew slowly in Len Milliard's eyes and his heavy face darkened with slow-rising anger. "I hope I didn't understand you," he said heavily. "I hope what I am thinking isn't true."

Sandson's smile grew wolfish. "Len," he said, "a man has to stay on one side or the other, and he should be willing to go along with his own side. With the Powells out of the way, someone else must handle the cattle-buying. You are the logical man. Think about it for a moment."

Len Milliard was thinking about it. Indecision showed

128

in his face. "We'll talk with you in the morning," the marshal said and, rising, led the mayor out of the house.

Once on the dark sidewalk Andrew Hyde spoke hoarsely, "That was a mistake. You said too much."

"I said exactly enough," Sandson corrected him. "The guilty knowledge will prey on Milliard, and the longer he fails to speak the more he will be bound to us. A man like Milliard is governed by his hope of gain. He won't speak out because, by doing so, he would lose his chance at the cattle-buying business. As long as the major is believed a murderer—that long will Milliard hold his peace. Every hour adds to his guilt for not speaking out."

Hyde looked at his companion. "Sometimes, Deacon, I think I don't know you at all."

"I'm not hard to know," said Sandson. "You and I made a pact, Andrew, when you hired me. You said then that you wanted certain things. I told you that I also wanted certain things, and if we worked together we could have them. Have I been wrong yet? The town is in our grasp. This part of the country is ours for the taking. There were only two men in our way. One is dead and his grangers are leaderless. The other is a hunted murderer."

"And what if Powell should ride in?"

"Let him," said Sandson. "I almost hope he does. He can do us no harm, since few will side with him."

"He might kill you."

"No," said Sandson. "He hesitates, and a man who hesitates never stands a fair chance with a man who knows what he is after and is willing to fight for it. Good night." He turned abruptly then and left the mayor staring after him as he moved across the street and stepped into the lobby of the hotel.

It was typical of Deacon Sandson that, although his first impulse on hitting town had been to hunt up Jenny Paraine, he put off their meeting until he had completed those things which he felt needed doing.

He had an orderly mind and an iron control which governed his actions, and he almost never did anything on sheer impulse. John Kleban was behind the desk posting his books. He looked up as Sandson came in, and the fleeting expression which crossed his face was not one of pleasure.

"When did you hit town?"

"An hour ago."

"What's the news?"

"Good," said Sandson. "The farmers are whipped. I hit Daigle's camp and destroyed it. His men are dead or scattered."

The hotelkeeper showed surprise. "Why Daigle?"

"He was siding with the grangers," Sandson told him. "With Que Layton dead Daigle might well have stepped in to lead them. I don't think he will now."

John Kleban was not satisfied. He was too smart a man not to sense that there was more behind Sandson's action than appeared on the surface. "And Daigle?" he asked. "You kill him?"

A hint of anger crept into Sandson's even tone. "He got away. I've still got four men in the hills hunting him. They'll find him if he doesn't ride clear out of the country." His eyes told plainly that the men would not bring Daigle in alive.

"And the major?" Kleban changed the subject. "What's this talk of murder?"

"It's not talk," said Sandson. "Powell left us to circle through the hills. Apparently he crept up on the back of Layton's camp and knifed old Que. I've got to give him credit. It broke the farmers as nothing else would have done. But we can't have open murder. We'll have to try to hang him if he's ever caught. My guess is that he rode out of the country, he and that fat printer."

Kleban lowered his eyes to the ledger to mask his thoughts from the watching marshal. He did not for a single minute believe that Bruce Powell had murdered Layton. Had the big granger been killed in a fair fight he would have had no doubts; but he had watched the major for three months and judged him fully.

Nor did it strike him as odd that in one breath Sandson could admit hunting Daigle down and in the next prattle about catching a murderer. The man was consistent only in following his own purposes. But Kleban had no intention of picking a fight with Sandson, and held his peace.

The marshal was hesitating now. "I know it's late, but I'd like to talk to Jenny. Will you call her or should I go up to her room?"

Kleban hesitated. He knew the girl did not wish to see Sandson or talk to him, but prudence kept him from crossing the deacon.

"I'll call her," he said and climbed the stairs.

34.

JENNY PARAINE came down into the lobby slowly. She had been asleep and she had dressed hurriedly at Kleban's call, thinking Henry Powell had taken a turn for the worse. Not until she stepped into the upper hall had she realized that it was Sandson who waited for her.

Then her impulse had been to turn back into her room and bar the door; but she forced herself to move to the stairs and down them to the lobby below.

John Kleban did not follow. Instead he turned into Henry Powell's room and found the doctor dozing beside the wounded man's bed. Henry was sleeping heavily. He did not rouse at Kleban's entrance, but Horndyke's eyes came open. He looked at the hotel-man questioningly.

"Sandson's downstairs," Kleban told him in an undertone, "looking like the cat that just ate the mouse. The man jumped Daigle's camp and scattered the crew. He says it was because Daigle might lead the farmers now that Layton's dead, but if you ask me he was after the boy."

Horndyke nodded, glancing toward the bed. "Did he get him?"

"Apparently not. Nor Daigle either, for that matter. But he still has four men out in the hills looking."

"And Powell? What of him?"

"He's not been caught either. Sandson believes—or pretends to believe—that Powell has run."

"He'd better," said Horndyke. "If he comes back to the Springs he'll hang. The young Laytons and their farmer friends will see to that even if Sandson doesn't."

"But you don't think he'll run?"

Horndyke considered. "That's hard to say. The human mind is a tricky thing. A stupid man puts down his head and charges like a bull. A smart man tries to figure some way to avoid the need of the charge. Where's Sandson now?"

"With Jenny, in the lobby."

"There's your answer," said Horndyke, and sighed. "I

131

don't think the major would run away. He's not the running kind. But he might try and find some legal way of fighting Sandson if it wasn't for the girl. She changes everything, her being here, and Sandson's after her. No, Bruce Powell will come riding in, and I for one will like to stand by and help him if I can."

Kleban didn't answer. He opened the door to listen, and the faint murmur of the voices below stairs came up to greet him.

Jenny Paraine had paused on the lower step so that her head was just on a level with Sandson, who still stood against the desk.

"You wanted to see me?"

It was Sandson's impulse to cross the space which separated them and take her in his arms. The fires of his desire glowed in his odd-colored eyes and brought an involuntary shiver to the girl.

"Of course, I wanted to see you." His tone sounded a little thick. "I've wanted nothing else since you first came to the Springs."

"Please, don't." She put out one hand as if to fend him off, although he had not moved.

"Listen," he said, and there was a roughness in his tone which he had never used to her before. "I tried to get your boy last night. I shot up Daigle's camp. We killed half a dozen men and the rest lit out. Daigle got away. He took the boy with him, but I left four men in the hills, hunting them. Even now they may have Bobby, may be heading for the Springs."

"No . . ." She pressed her hand tightly against her mouth.

"You mean you don't want the boy?" The words burst from him incredulously.

"Want him? Of course I want him. But I don't want him that way. I don't want men slaughtered. I don't even wish Clayton Daigle dead."

"You're willy-nilly," he said. "You're like the major. You want things but you don't want to fight for them or pay what you have to pay. This is a hard country, Jenny, and things only come to those who are willing to fight and pay the price. Make up your mind, my dear. Say the word and I'll get that boy for you, even if I have to trail Daigle clear to Mexico—and I'm the only one who can. Don't pin your hopes on Powell. He'll hang. He'll hang the minute I give the sign."

132

"The minute you give the sign," she said. "He'll hang, when anyone who knows him knows that he can't possibly be guilty? That's clever of you, Deacon." Some of the fear had gone out of her voice. "You were afraid of him, so you took this way to get him out of your way."

"Afraid?" Deacon Sandson stared at her, insulted by the suggestion. "You think I'm afraid of Bruce Powell?"

"What else can I think when you choose this underhanded way of getting rid of him?"

"Ah," he said, "so you think I was afraid to face him. How little you know me. I'll prove it to you, Jenny. I'll show you, since that's what you wish." He turned then and stalked from the hotel, leaving the girl standing at the bottom of the stairs looking after him.

She stood there for a long time, and then she whispered, "Bruce, what have I done to you now? I've put a crazy killer on your trail. What little chance you had before is gone. Sandson will never stop until he finds you, until one of you is dead." She sank down on the lower step, burying her face in her cradled arm, and thus John Kleban found her when he came down into the lobby a quarter of an hour later.

35.

IT WAS after five o'clock the next afternoon when John Kleban left the hotel. Crossing the railroad tracks, he came into Frenchy Armaud's place and found the saloon's proprietor against his own bar.

Armaud showed his surprise at the unexpected visitor by arching his eyebrows slightly, and indicated his office door with a little motion of his head. Once inside, Kleban came to the point at once.

"Have you heard anything from Bruce Powell?"

Armaud drew a long, crooked cheroot from the pocket of his ornate vest and lit it carefully before he answered. "And what makes you believe that I would have heard from Powell?"

Kleban was strangely embarrassed. "You have been friendly with the Powells," he said slowly. "I have an idea

133

that he would trust you sooner than he would trust anyone else in town."

Frenchy's mustache lifted at one corner as he gave Kleban a cynical grin. "You are not the only one to have that idea, my friend. The marshal has had a man watching this place all day."

"I know," said Kleban, "and I did not want you to get the idea that I was playing Sandson's game. Andrew Hyde and Len Milliard are, although Milliard has bucked over the traces to the point where he allowed Sandson only the expense of four deputies. The rest are taking the evening train east. Milliard says that four men should handle Powell if he shows up, especially since the Layton boys and the farmers will be on hand to back them up."

Frenchy, who already had this information from his private sources, showed no surprise. But he did arch his brows when Kleban added, "I wouldn't be here, but I thought I saw someone at the print shop early this morning, and some food was stolen from my kitchen during the night."

"You don't tell me."

The hotelkeeper looked at Armaud suspiciously, but the Frenchman's face was bland. "You think perhaps it was the major?"

"I don't know what to think," Kleban admitted. "If it is, just tell him that I'll be in the lobby, and if he needs an extra gun I'll be around." He turned then and moved out the door and shut it quietly after him. Armaud remained where he was, twisting the thin cigar between his lips, staring at nothing in particular.

At nine-thirty a man slipped into Frenchy's office and nodded. "He's here."

Frenchy turned from the desk. "Anyone see him?"

The man shook his head. "I met him a mile down the road. We didn't use the bridge coming in. We forded the river. I brought him up through the alley. He's in the storeroom."

Frenchy rose. He almost never wore a gun, not figuring that he was expert enough with firearms, that it was the other fellow's game, to be let strictly alone. But now he pulled a belt from the desk and buckled it about his hips. Lifting a forty-four from the drawer, he spun the cylinder and dropped it into the empty holster. That done, he buttoned the long-tailed coat and followed the man into the main saloon.

The big room was filled and noisy, and he moved between

the crowded tables with no sign of haste, pausing here and there to speak to one of the gamblers. Then he reached the rear door and stepped through into the storeroom.

Bruce Powell sat on an upended box, still dirty from the trail and unshaved. His eyes were red-rimmed from fatigue, but the pupils were clear and alert. He rose, without words, shook Armaud's hand, then sat down again.

"It was a good idea, meeting me on the trail. Thanks."

"The marshal has had this place watched all day," Frenchy said. "I didn't think it fair to you to step into trouble the instant you hit town."

"The sooner the better," Bruce Powell said. "I've learned something in the last few days. Sometimes you have to meet force with force head-on. Sometimes there isn't any other way, and the longer you put it off the worse things get."

"That's true," said Armaud, "but I have something to show you first." He walked to the corner of the room, shoved some boxes aside and raised a trap door.

"Cappy, it's me."

"Ah," said Cappy Ayers, "and it's pleasing to see a light. I never was meant to be a mole. Come down."

Bruce Powell had risen to his feet. "Cappy!" He crossed the room quickly and dropped down into the small rock-walled cellar. Frenchy followed, carrying the lamp. The cellar was only eight feet square and a good part of it was filled with whiskey kegs. Between two of the kegs a folded blanket had been placed on the earth floor and Bobby Daigle slept peacefully.

Bruce Powell stared at the small boy and said under his breath, "Well, what do you know! Where did you find him, Cappy?"

"On a hilltop," the fat man said, "above where Daigle's camp was before Sandson hit them."

"So, it was you? There were the tracks of two horses . . ."

"Lefty James." Cappy was grinning. "You didn't think I'd have found the place all by myself? That James can track better than an Indian."

"When did you get in here?"

"Last night. James came in with me and we raided the hotel kitchen. We stopped at the print shop, but I didn't figure the boy would be safe there, so I brought him down here. Did you ever try to keep a four-year-old cooped up in a place this small for a full day? He done wore me out."

Powell grinned slightly. "Where's James?"

"He's camped a couple of miles downriver," Cappy said. "He's got a couple of men with him, friends of his that were riding with Sandson. We ran into them in the hills. The deacon had left them out there, hunting for the boy."

"So?" Powell knew there was something else to tell. Cappy was grinning happily. "Let's have it."

"They've got another man with them," Cappy said. "Fellow named Jordan. Seems like we borrowed a few bottles of whiskey along with the food. Seems like this Jordan drank a wee bit too much. He got quarrelsome and then he got to bragging. He claims he's killed eight men and got notches in his gun to prove it. He pulled his knife and started on another notch and they asked him who that one was for. He said Que Layton."

There was silence in the little cellar. Powell stared at the fat man and then at Frenchy.

"Jordan's tied up," Cappy said. "Lefty will keep him out there until we send word."

Bruce Powell let out his breath slowly. "I thought you and Lefty were riding out of the country?"

"We started," Cappy said. "We must have gone a good fifteen miles before we camped. And in the morning we got up and saddled the horses and mounted. And then durned if both of us didn't turn around, not saying a word, and ride back. We found Daigle's camp burned out, and then James found tracks coming down the creek and taking off toward the south—a man, walking."

"Mine."

"Probably. Anyhow, we backtracked up the creek and found the boy. We hadn't gone more than two miles until we ran into these jaspers Sandson had left to search the hills. I thought for sure our goose was cooked, but as I said, two of them was friends of Lefty, and this Jordan didn't say a word. He was a silent cuss until he got that liquor in him and then he talked all over his face."

"Which won't do any good," said Frenchy Armaud, "as long as Sandson is marshal. Sober, this killer is going to deny ever having confessed. If James and the boys brought him in, Sandson would see that he was turned loose. The farmers believe you're a murderer, Major. They want to believe it, and Sandson wants them to. The best thing for you and Cappy to do is to slip away. You'll never get a fair trial in Dexter Springs."

Bruce Powell turned to look at him. "I'm not going anywhere," he said. "This is between Sandson and me. There's no longer any other answer."

Frenchy Armaud did not argue. Cappy said quickly, "Don't be a fool, Major. You can't step out onto the street. You'd never have a chance. You'd be bucking another man's game, and only a crazy man does that."

Powell didn't answer. Instead, he said, "Does Jenny know that the boy is safe?"

"She does not," said Cappy. "I haven't dared stir from here, and if Frenchy had sent a man uptown to see her it would have been a tip-off. They've been watching this place constantly. You don't think I wanted my head stuck in a noose? Don't forget, I was with you the night Que Layton was knifed."

Powell nodded slowly. He stooped, gathered up the sleeping boy, wrapping the blanket around him carefully. The child stirred, whimpered a little but did not wake. Powell turned toward the ladderlike stairs and climbed back to the storeroom. Cappy and Armaud followed, Cappy carrying his shotgun.

"If you're crazy enough to walk up to the hotel, why, so am I."

"No, you don't," said Powell. "But there is one thing you two can do." He turned to the Frenchman. "You say there's a man watching the saloon?"

Armaud nodded.

"See if you can put a gun on him and bring him back here. Cappy can keep him in the cellar for a while. I'd just as soon get to the hotel without Sandson knowing I'm in town."

36.

CARRYING THE blanketed boy, Bruce Powell moved quickly along the railroad track to where the alley dead-ended against the grade. He dropped down into its shadows and moved along the ruts, past the rear door of Quince's livery, past his print shop and Len Milliard's store, and so reached the entrance of the hotel kitchen.

The room was in darkness as was the dining room beyond. He crossed them, pushed the lobby door open a crack and peered through. No one was in the lobby. He stepped in and moved quickly toward the stairs.

He had gained them and was starting upward when the door from the bar opened and a man came halfway through. He stopped, seeing Powell, and surprise held him motionless for the instant. Then he stepped back into the bar, shouting as he did so.

"It's Powell! It's the major! He's here, in the hotel!"

Powell cursed under his breath and ran quickly up the stairs and along the hall to Jenny Paraine's room. He did not even pause to knock. He tried the knob and, finding the door unlocked, thrust it inward.

Jenny Paraine had been asleep. She roused as the door swung open and came up on one elbow, saying quickly, "Doctor, what is it?"

"It's not Horndyke," Bruce Powell said, and was already beside the bed. "It's me, Jenny. I've brought you Bobby." He put the boy on the bed at her side.

Jenny Paraine's mind was so drugged with sleep that it was hard for her to grasp the words.

"Bruce! Bobby!" She clutched the boy to her convulsively.

"Daigle's dead," he said. "There's no reason now why you can't have the boy—but listen to me, for I only have a minute. Get up, get dressed and pack. There's a train east at five-thirty in the morning. Get Kleban to put you on it. No matter what happens, get on that train."

"Bruce!" She was fully awake now. "How did you get here? Were you seen?"

"I was seen," he said grimly.

"Then you've got to go. Sandson means to kill you. He won't even bring you to trial. That's my fault. He thinks I believe him a coward. He's going to prove to me that he's not. He's going to prove it by killing you." She shuddered. "Everything I do seems to bring you more trouble. I'm a jinx. I have been since the first moment you saw me."

"You're wonderful," he said and kissed her hard, her arms coming up around his neck to hold his bearded face down against her.

"Maybe it isn't too late," she said. "You can slip out the back way. We can meet somewhere, anywhere you name. We can . . ."

He broke the hold of her arms and straightened. "It is too

late," he told her. "Ever since the war I've been, in effect, running from things, but I can't run any more. I've got to face this thing out, no matter what happens."

"He'll kill you," she said frantically. "He's a devil, Bruce."

"Maybe," he said, "but dying isn't so terrible, Jenny. It's the way you die. Someone has to stop Sandson. I guess the job is mine." He backed toward the door, then paused. "How's Henry?"

"Getting better," she said. "It was touch and go, but Horndyke says he'll get well. He's in the second room."

Powell slipped out into the hall. He moved quickly to the door of his brother's room and peered in. Edna Layton sat beside the bed, dozing in her chair. He did not wake her, but her presence brought a warm, quick smile to his lips. He closed the door softly and went to the head of the stairs.

Men's voices reached him from below. "I tell you he's up there. He's probably with his brother. Let's get him."

"Not me." It was a stranger's voice. "Wait for Sandson. I'm not going up those stairs against any armed killer . . ."

Powell turned and faded back along the hall. There was a window at the alley end. He raised it, peered through into the darkness below; then, letting himself over the sill, dropped lightly to the rutted ground.

He stood for a moment in the deep shadow of the building, listening. Satisfied, he turned and moved through the side alley which ran out to the street between the hotel and Milliard's store.

State Street was deserted. He paused, looking up and down its wide expanse, then moved sidewise so he had the store at his back.

He stopped then, leaning against one of the posts which supported the wooden awning, and waited. From where he stood he had a full view of the street, and no one could get behind him unless they came through the store.

To his left he could hear faintly the voices of the men in the hotel. To his right there was sound from the dives below the railroad. But the rest of the night was quiet.

He waited. It was not the first time he had stood in the darkness waiting thus for death. He had done the same thing a dozen times during the war. But then there had been others around him, and the nervous restlessness of waiting had been shared. Now he was alone, and he had no idea of what the odds against him might be. The marshal might come alone or with a dozen men at his back.

He waited, and he had a chance to think of his brother, of their plans and hopes for this town, of Jenny and the boy. He had time to wonder what would become of them—and then he saw Sandson.

The marshal came out of the grange hall, and he came alone, moving quickly toward the hotel as if he had been summoned there by a messenger. Men came out of the grange hall behind him, but they stopped, and Bruce Powell remembered Jenny's words, 'He believes I think him a coward. He's going to prove me wrong by killing you.'

Sandson was coming alone because he wished it that way. To a man of his vanity there could be no question of aid; nor did the marshal believe that he needed help. He had supreme confidence in his speed and his ability.

He stepped up onto the hotel gallery, and his hand was extended toward the door when Powell's voice stopped him.

"Here," said the major. "I'm here, Deacon, waiting for you."

He moved sidewise then, out of the shadow into the moonlight of the street. He stood there, facing the hotel, his hands hanging loosely at his sides. For a moment he remembered that only a little time before, he and the deacon had faced each other in nearly the same place, and that then he had refused the deacon's challenge. He wondered what difference that refusal had made.

Que Layton might still have been alive and the farmers still holding the Sand Hills against the herds. But he put the thought away from him almost as quickly as it came, giving his full attention to the man on the hotel porch.

Sandson had stopped at the first sound of the major's voice. For a moment he stood motionless, his hand still holding the half-open door. Then he let the hand fall to his side. He turned deliberately, stalked to the edge of the porch and stepped downward into the street.

He stopped then, facing the major, some fifteen feet separating them.

"I want you," he said, "for the murder of Que Layton. Put your hands in the air."

"Always careful," Powell's voice came mockingly through the quiet night. The hotel door behind the marshal had filled with men, as had the bar entrance and the fronting windows.

"The murder story has played out," Powell said. "We

140

have the man who used my knife. The man you paid to kill Layton. Jordan has already talked, Sandson. You'll have to choose another way."

"Like this, then," the deacon said, and his right hand swept downward toward his hip. It seemed to rise almost at once, bringing up the heavy gun.

Bruce Powell made no effort to hurry his draw. He was fast, but he knew the deacon was faster. He was much more concerned with hitting his target than with the speed in which he brought up the twin guns.

The deacon fired first, his gun exploding almost before it was clear of the holster, the bullet striking the mud five feet in front of Powell. His second shot hit the major in the chest, the shocking power of the heavy bullet almost knocking him from his feet.

He fought to steady himself as the deacon's third bullet clipped the shoulder of his brush jacket—and then both his guns went off, the shots so closely spaced that it was a continuous hammer of explosive sound.

He saw Sandson sway, saw the man's arm drop, saw him take a step forward and then lurch down onto his face. Powell's fingers ceased to squeeze the triggers. He stood perfectly still, afraid to move lest he fall down. He watched the deacon intently but Sandson was motionless.

Men had flooded out onto the hotel porch, and others were pouring down the street from the direction of the grange hall. And suddenly Frenchy Armaud and Cappy Ayers came out of the alley at a half-run, followed by John Kleban. Both Cappy and Kleban had shotguns, while Frenchy carried a heavy rifle.

Cappy planted himself in the middle of the street in front of Powell, his shotgun menacing the men on the porch.

"Get back, all of you!"

Kleban was at his side, his shotgun backing up the fat printer. Armaud put a hand on Powell's shoulder. "You hit?"

"In the chest," Powell said, and was surprised that he could speak.

"Get him back to the print shop." It was Cappy, still watching the men on the street.

Armaud put an arm under Powell's and turned him around. The major's legs seemed to be made of rubber. "I'll never make it," he muttered.

Armaud wasted no breath in argument. He stooped and

caught the major up in his arms. His thick, squat body was surprisingly strong, and he carried the hundred and ninety pounds without faltering.

It was dark in the shop, and they made no effort to light the lamps. Kleban and Cappy had retreated after them, walking backward, still covering the street until they slipped through the door.

Armaud had set the major against the high counter. He stood there, refusing to sit down, his guns still in his hands. "You three duck out the back way." His voice sounded stronger, as if he were controlling it with his will. "Those farmers from the grange hall will be flooding down here in a minute and then you can't get out."

"Hell with it," said Cappy. He used the barrel of his gun to shatter one of the windows. "We'll make them kind of unhappy before they get to us."

"Go on." Bruce Powell holstered one of his guns and used his free hand to load the other. "I'll take care of myself. There's no need the rest of you staying."

He got no answer. Frenchy Armaud had moved to the rear door. Kleban was at the second front window. From where they stood they had a good view of the men who were slowly moving down the street. They reached the marshal's body, halted, surrounding it, then picked him up and carried him toward the hotel bar. The rest turned and came on slowly toward the print shop. At a hundred feet they halted and one man stepped out, the white cloth sling that held his arm marking him. It was Pete Layton.

"Powell! Can you hear me?"

"We're not deaf," Cappy called back.

"All right," said the boy. "We'll give you a chance to step out, Major. The others can go. We want you."

"Come and get him," said Cappy, raising the shotgun. "This is full of nuts and bolts. See how you like them."

The crowd wavered a little. Pete Layton never moved. "I'll remember you," he told the printer, "but first Powell. We'll get you if we have to burn this place."

Someone behind him in the crowd fired, the bullet singing through the window past Cappy's head.

"Why damn you," said Cappy and let go with both barrels.

There were yells from the crowd. One man went down, but struggled back to his feet and joined the scramble up the street.

142

Cappy was reloading and there was marked satisfaction in his voice. "That'll show them."

"Not for long," Powell told him as a sniper's bullet cut through the door and zinged off the metal frame of the press. "You can't hope to hold them off. They can cut down at us from any direction, or they can fire the building from the roof of Milliard's store." He interrupted himself to snap a shot at a man trying to poke a gun around the corner of the window.

"You better get out now."

"Nuts," said Cappy, and shot up the street.

Suddenly there was a crash of guns from across the street. Kleban swore softly and sat down, his gun slipping from his grasp.

Bruce Powell started forward. "You hit, John?"

"Keep back, only an arm." The hotelman was already fumbling for his fallen gun.

And then there was a yell from the lower end of the street. A group of riders charged across the railroad and swept up toward the print shop.

Cappy gripped his gun tighter, saying grimly, "Looks like they've got horses. Looks like they mean to ride us down."

Bruce Powell shouted at him suddenly, "Careful! Don't shoot. Those aren't farmers. Those are Texas yells."

"Well, damn me." Cappy was leaning out the window, contemptuous of the marksman up the street. "It looks like Downer. It is Downer! Hey, Wirt! This way. This way!"

The riders swerved and pulled up before the shop. The small trail boss was out of the saddle at once and stomping into the dark room.

"Where's Powell?"

Bruce Powell's legs had folded under him. He was sitting on the floor, his back to the high counter. "Welcome to Dexter Springs." He grinned faintly in the darkness. "You'll never know quite how welcome you are."

Downer said dryly, "We heard the shooting before we crossed the river. I got the notion you might need help."

"I did," Powell told him. "But what are you doing here?"

The trail boss shrugged. "After you rode out this morning the boys got to talking. And finally we left four men to hold the herd and rode on in just in case. What do you want us to do, run these jaspers out of town?"

143

Powell looked out to where the riders had thrown a skirmish line across the street. Above them, before the hotel, the farmers were collecting slowly. As he watched, Len Milliard and Andrew Hyde pushed through to the mounted men and after a momentary argument came on into the shop.

"Whose men are these?" It was the mayor, sounding pompous as always.

"Mine," said Wirt Downer. "Who are you?"

Hyde ignored him, for he had seen Powell. "Major," he crossed to the seated man, "this shooting has to stop."

"We're willing," said Cappy. "Talk to the farmers."

"I intend to." The mayor looked back at Powell, and embarrassment grew in his tone. "I've already been trying to talk to them. Sandson is dead. I've told them both Milliard and I are convinced that you did not murder Que Layton."

Powell stared at him. "What are you talking about?"

The mayor hesitated. "Both Milliard and I got the idea that Sandson had something to do with the murder." He sounded more embarrassed than ever. "To be truthful, we've both been afraid of Sandson, afraid to oppose him . . ."

Cappy spat. "A fine bunch. Of course Sandson arranged Que Layton's killing. We've got the man he hired to stab Layton with the major's knife, but we couldn't bring him into town as long as Sandson lived . . ."

He broke off, for Jenny Paraine had run down the alley and came bursting in the rear door. A moment later Horndyke puffed after her.

"Bruce!" She dropped at his side. "Are you all right?"

"All right," he said, and tried to rise. He failed, but it did not matter. She slipped both arms about his neck, pressing her wet cheek to his.

"Here," said Horndyke. "Here, that's no way to treat a wounded man." But neither of them heard him, and even if they had, neither would have cared.

THE END